# Almond Apparition

Endru Atros

***

ORIGINALLY PUBLISHED IN POLAND AS MIGDALOWA ZJAWA

***

TRANSLATED AND PUBLISHED IN ENGLISH WITH PERMISSION.

***

PAPERBACK ISBN: 978-1-7363485-3-6

EPUB ISBN: 978-1-3930051-5-5

***

WRITTEN BY ENDRU ATROS

PUBLISHED BY ROYAL HAWAIIAN PRESS

COVER ART BY TYRONE ROSHANTHA

TRANSLATED BY ROLAND TURNER

PUBLISHING ASSISTANCE: DOROTA RESZKE

***

FOR MORE WORKS BY THIS AUTHOR, PLEASE VISIT:

WWW.ROYALHAWAIIANPRESS.COM

***

VERSION NUMBER 1.0

Canadian submarine HMCS Corner Brook, SSK-878 - twin of HMCS Corner Drak, SSK-264

Somewhere off the coast of Canada

# Prolog

The story of the "Kursk", a Russian hi-tech nuclear submarine that sank on August 12, 2000, about 100 miles from the Murmansk naval base is well known. The entire crew and visiting officers of the Northern Fleet Staff died then. What did the sailors feel and think about, trapped in its steel hull?

We'll never know that.

Some of the sailors survived the sinking of a Canadian submarine, and Polish rescuers who fought for their lives will tell us the story of the rescue operation which will have its continuation on Canadian soil. There, love and emotions intertwine with the great enigma of a mysterious underwater rock cliff.

The story of this ship is based in part on facts.

Endru Atros

# Chapter I

## HMCS SSK-264

***Tuesday, August 4***

The dark shadow of the ship glided beneath the surface in the chilled waters of the Labrador Sea. The crew in the machine room cursed the captain and his penchant for making the "Crazy Vasily" loop. All the loose things put away now littered the corners of the engine room.

"The submarine is not a carousel to make figures like in a training plane! Harry," the second mechanic, was angry, bending down to get the keys stuck somewhere between the steel gratings.

They had been sailing for sixteen hours on a Level II alarm. According to the procedures, all hatches separating individual watertight bulkheads should be closed, but they were not, because the increased traffic of sailors leaving the service and changing their colleagues from the evening watch caused a delay in sealing the next rooms. It was the middle of the night when a sudden explosion beneath the main engine startled all crew members within its range. The stern was lifted up, and all of them, thrown by its mighty force, fell, hitting various machines, pipes and other steel parts of the ship. Before its rear part had even fallen, a huge wave of orange-yellow fire appeared. It glided down from the bottom of the ship, swirling and filling every nook and cranny of the rooms. It mowed everything with great speed and everyone on its way. They didn't stand a chance.

Those who lost consciousness from hitting some hard metal parts of the ship died in the blink of an eye without realizing it. A dozen or so above the machinery deck torn apart by the explosion started to flee, but they had no way of saving them. The fire with its destructive force, magnified by the small dimensions of the rooms, was moving faster than their escape ability. Caught in a flame of a temperature of above a thousand degrees, they died in great pain and suffering. The shockwave of the blast, rolling through all the open rooms in the stern section, stopped in the closed command compartment. Immediately behind it, the violently penetrating water extinguished the spreading fire and increased the air pressure, flooding the entire aft part. It poured rapidly into all the rooms of the engine room, mess rooms and their cabins, drowning the remaining sailors. The opened battery compartment disappeared under water in a few seconds. Fortunately, the upper, last compartment of the ship from the side of the conning tower was closed. Behind it were nineteen crew members in the command part, and two decks below, at the very prow in the torpedo compartment, thirty-eight men froze in terror. An air trap has formed in their room and in two adjoining rooms. This air from the entire ship "escaped" to the forward, uppermost part of the ship, and squeezed by the pouring water, equalized the pressure that existed at that depth, stopping its further influx.

"How long will we have enough air?" Many of them asked themselves this question.

Twenty-two hours earlier, a ciphertext arrived at the Canadian Navy's military base.

The flagship commander of the Port Naomi combat team read the deciphered order:

*Commander of the Battle Ship Flotilla, Commander Peter Wilson – Go to the KONDOR area, locate an enemy submarine heading for Canadian territory from the Labrador Sea. Don't let the rockets fire. Make it emergence or sink it.*

*Commander of the Royal Canadian Navy, Admiral Alex Windsor.*

In the port, all the military units on standby threw their lines and went out to sea one by one. On the orders of the commander of the V 354 missile destroyer (Polar explorer), commander of the entire flotilla, the entire armada formed a combat formation and moved with the full power of its machines to the given area. After sixteen hours of sailing in formation, the ships began to move away from each other, creating an ever-widening semicircle. Their goal was to penetrate as much water as possible, in which the enemy ship could disappear. It was as if they had spread a huge net at first, with the remaining combat units leading left and right - the two destroyers. Two anti-submarine helicopters took off for the air patrol. Their target was an unidentified submarine. Meanwhile, in the cold waters of the North Atlantic, the SSK-264, sailing at a depth of 350 meters, took a course for a group of islets between the Greenland headland

and the entrance to Canada. Its position was located a day earlier. The hydroacoustic buoy dropped from the plane caught it in its embrace, so the commander realized that he had been targeted and now his only chance is to outsmart the enemy, because he has no chance in direct combat.

"It's still tracking us," Big Ear reported sixteen hours ago.

Having made the "Crazy Vasyl" loop, the SSK-264 submarine set off countercourse towards the nearby islands.

The master seaman Big Ear - as they called him in the fleet - had remarkable ability to hear and distinguish sounds for others that were a cluster of noise, whistles or crackles. It was his unusual idea that was applied to this ship. Acoustic signals with a frequency of 10 to 40 Hz were used to track and locate enemy ships. The scale of these signals was confusingly similar to the sounds made by blue whales. Only a highly trained ear will be able to distinguish the natural singing of a whale from the acoustic signal they send. On a submarine, ears replace eyes. Here you see the sounds - whoever can distinguish faster and more accurately what sounds he is dealing with, wins the battle. Direct clash of two submarines in peacetime involves constant control of a potential enemy.

Contrary to appearances, the submarine is not able to hide. It may lurk for some time somewhere in the depths, in some rocky fork or a deep underwater gorge. But as soon as it moves on the sound of its engines and propellers running will be picked up and recognized by one of the numerous hydrophone lying on the seabed or at a certain depth.

Therefore, submarines use various tricks to confuse the enemy. The specialty of the SSK-264 was to pretend to be a whale, or more precisely - a blue whale. Its specific low-frequency but high-intensity singing is perhaps one of the loudest sounds that an animal living on earth makes. The 188 dBA he can deliver is intended to communicate with other whales. And they made such sounds. The specialist devices at their disposal were able to "hear" this sound even from a distance of 800 kilometers, which has been a phenomenon on a global scale so far. They always knew where the whales were. They developed a speed of 18 knots - the maximum they could achieve while underwater. After the "Crazy Vasily" maneuver, they found themselves under the very surface of the ocean, in a group of cetaceans swimming nearby. The depth rudders were set at forty meters. They were in a hurry, they wanted to reach the land as quickly as possible, where the underwater Labrador stream bends in a wide arc, colliding with the Gulf of the North Atlantic - that was their goal. They wanted to hide there. Turn off the engines and let themself be carried away by its power. Not far from where they were, enormous masses of water plunged into the fault of the rock and - guided by its rock face - plunged into the depths of the ocean. The captain had all the signal buoys deactivated - just in case they had to make sudden maneuvers. It already happened to them that during a sudden turn while escaping from the training torpedo pursuing them, the buoy, subjected to a greater load, broke free and surfaced, with a timid chirp, sending a call for rescue and thus announcing their position to everyone around them. Then they dropped out of further exercises. Command deemed them "hit and sunk." There was no explanation that it was not their fault, only the inadequate security of the rescue buoys - the shame remained in their minds for a long time. The ship's commander, Harry Montery, sat in his command seat.

"How are the signals still tracking us?" says to the petty officer Big Ear.

"No, they don't catch us in their tentacles anymore, but they know our previous direction," Big Ear replies, taking the receiver off one ear for a moment.

"Course 250 degrees," it's to the helmsman.

"Keep depth. Report distance to land."

The First Officer places a new position on the map.

"We will get the electricity in 2 minutes," he reports.

Then a massive explosion rocked the ship. The captain was thrown from his armchair onto the far wall, he fell and hit his head against the edge of the sonar cabinet. The loss of consciousness deprived the commander's crew. All lights went off, all monitors and navigation devices turned off. A terrifying silence fell on the ship. Two dim hazard lights glowed faintly, flashing red and yellow nervously. The only sound was the water pouring into the ship. The air pressure began to increase rapidly, making their ears ache.

"We're drowning!" Someone shouted from the darkness.

The fearful scream prompted the lieutenant to act. Sitting at the depth controls, he managed to stay in his seat without hitting anything hard. The first one also regained consciousness.

"Close the front compartment!" He shouted loudly. The two seamen closest started to bolt the open steel gates. When they left the command compartment, they sealed the compartment by quickly tightening the swivel. At the front, the locks of the bolts clicked, snapping into the pawls.

"Front compartment closed!" One of them shouted and ran back to the command compartment, covering his mouth and nose with his hand.

Behind them, in the room they closed, a trail of black smoke was already running. The other two jumped in, panting for breath.

"We did it!" One wheezed, coughing violently.

"Report the situation!" The lieutenant took command.

They screamed in vain at the microphone, calling out the individual compartments. Nobody spoke up.

"Report attendance!" The lieutenant ordered.

One by one, they announced the rank and function, adding "healthy", "I'm fine" or "I think my leg is broken."

The injured were immediately taken care of by the on-board doctor with a paramedic, putting on bandages and stiffening broken limbs. None of the compartments still answered the calls. In less than three minutes another burst shook the ship over and over explosions.

"The battery compartment above the engine room is on fire!" The Chief's voice was heard, the mechanic. Technical gas cylinders started to explode.

"How are the torpedoes?" The commander asked, regaining consciousness.

"Safe so far. Apparently they have closed the compartment. The last two emergency lights went out. Fire or water reached their batteries. We no longer have any power."

"What was that?" The sailor dared to ask.

"Torpedo, they hit us with a torpedo," it was heard from the end of the steward's compartment.

"No, definitely not," said Big Ear. "I'd hear its move."

"Then what was that? Hear something weird?" Some trembling voice asked from a distance.

"No, nothing at all - just cetaceans singing. No other noise, except for the training depth bombs dropped by our minesweepers in the designated area. But it's far away, because it's in the CONDOR area."

"Where did we get hit, how you think?" Big Ear asked this time.

"In the engine room, at the very bottom under the machine," answered the navigational helmsman, "we were thrown as if someone had torn the stern up by the screw. The prow bent sharply to the bottom. Then it straightened."

"What could it be?" Regaining consciousness, the captain spoke softly, more to himself than to his crew.

Silence answered him. Nobody asked the question - what next? What to do now?

They waited for orders - but there weren't any. They were locked up, cut off from the rest of the ship's quarters with no way of contacting the outside world - and at their own request.

Does fate have to be so cruel? Disaster strikes them when they turn off their own emergency signaling.

"Will they look for us?" The captain wondered. "Of course they will be, but not as a sunken submarine that needs immediate help, but as a perfectly camouflaged opponent of naval exercises," he replied to himself. "Am I the only one aware of this?"

"Time, how much time do we have?" Someone said from across the room.

The captain recognized the watchman's voice. This is Alan, a young blue jacket who is making the first cruise on a submarine. They were supposed to be baptized of fire after the exercises, now they don't have to, if they survive, it will be his real baptism, he thought sadly.

Silence, frightening silence means death of the other seamen. Radzik keeps calling individual compartments. But they don't answer. So?

This dark thought cuts his consciousness to the point of pain.

"It's my fault?" A sense of failure ran through his whole body. "Did I kill them?" He wondered. From these dark reflections the voice of the First broke him:

"Captain... We are still sailing..."

"Indeed, I sense the movement of the ship," confirmed his observation. "The rudders work? The rudder emergency system works?" He called to the steersman.

"No! Nothing works, everything is locked in the position they were in when they exploded," both helmsmen reply, one from the depth rudder and the other from the direction.

"Periscope?"

"Locked out!"

"Depth?"

"40 meters."

"Are we falling?"

"I suppose not anymore."

"What does that mean "I suppose"?"

"Cannot see, indicators are off," reports the lieutenant.

"But we have a light trim[1] to the stern, we probably take water," says Chief, engineer. A moment ago he put a rubber ball on the table, which he used to press while exercising the muscles of his hand. She rolled lightly towards his belly, which was resting against the table top and his back to the stern. He didn't need a light to know that.

The silence was disturbed by the rattle of the watchman's phone cranking, still hoping someone would answer his desperate attempts to make contact. This is the last chance to be contacted by phone. This phone did not need any power supply, it produced it by turning a crank. Hush, no one said anything.

"Fire team: take flashlights, put on apparatus with $CO_2$ absorbers and open the passage to beak.

[1] Trim - the ship's trim (in this case the stern was submerged more than the prow).

Check the next rooms. We need as much space as possible - the more open rooms, the more oxygen for us. Check whether it is possible to reach the magazine with oxygen devices."

"Execute!" the decisive order of the commander sounded.

"Two other watchkeepers: check emergency hatch. Flood and then empty the escape hatch."

"Aye aye!" He heard, and four faint shafts of light moved away towards their only hope of life.

They felt the ship veered slightly to the left. It is an underwater river, pushing them at the speed of a few knots, meeting a steep bottom in its path and turning sharply, racing down the underwater cliff. After a while, a strong blow of the prow against the bottom made everyone realize that they were lying motionless, thirty several meters under water. It tossed the stern a little more, because you could clearly hear the scraping of metal on the bottom. It is a lucky coincidence - if they had not hit the bottom here, the current would have carried them further, two hundred meters deep, and perhaps even deep into the nearby depths. The captain remembered the plan he wanted to test during these exercises. It's not too deep here - it could be worse. Some of them would be tempted to swim to the surface, but for what? There is no one there, and they would not have survived for four minutes without thermal suits in that icy water.

"Captain," two watchkeepers are reporting. "The evacuation system is operational. You can come to the surface."

After another five minutes, the other two sailors returned.

“We've opened another corridor, but the third compartment is terribly smoky, you can't leave it open. On the lower level, water, everything flooded, cannot reach the storage room with oxygen devices. Anyway, it is too far, and it is not known if it is blocked by something after the explosion."

"How much air will we have?" Asked the question from the darkness.

"We all have apparatus with CO2 absorbers," the First Officer said in reply.

"Who has not, report now."

Silence.

"Sit on deck and wait."

"I'm ordering a minute of silence," came the captain's voice.

"You have to find something for them to keep them from asking what if. Nobody knows how much air they have. We're using more of it because the ship has lost its zero decompression," he thought.

The silence lasted for several minutes. No thumps or other signs of life for the rest of the ship. It is impossible for anyone else to survive.

"Radzik, take something heavy and send a signal."

"Something heavy and pounding, but what and on what?" he thought irritated, "it was because of this smarty captain all the lifeboats were deactivated. He wanted to be the best in the fleet. If not for that, the rescue operation would have been going on a long time ago. Our chances of survival would be real. And now no one will help us, because it will not know that we need it urgent."

Someone handed him a large key to the door bolts.

"I guess the best thing to do is tap."

"But should I tap anything specific?" He thinks for a moment. "No... Nobody knows Morse code anyway."

So he bangs it on the door as much as he can, and the echo carries the sound around the room. Knock, knock, he repeats a few times and listens, and everyone present with him. He was about to start again when he heard the sound, the muffled but clear sound of the blows. Such chaotic but joyful pounding on some metal.

Then a few seconds of silence and steady beats, time and time again, at regular intervals.

Big Ear realized first.

"Five, six, seven," he began to count aloud, and after a while everyone was counting with him. Thirty-eight came out.

"The entire crew of the launchers and their free watches," said the lieutenant, "still eighteen missing, so thes are from the machine. Kitchen, wardroom and free watches. They had no chance. Everything from the stern to their compartment was destroyed by an explosion, fire and water."

"I must get them something to do," the captain thought, fearing the outbreak of collective panic.

"Everyone should remember what he was doing at the time of the blast and report to me one by one, from the deputy down," he ordered.

"I was taking position, we were close to land, about two cables from the shore. Unfortunately, the area is uninhabited. Wilderness," First Officer reported first.

"I was browsing the sailing directions and timing to influencing the Labrador stream," said the Third Officer, for the Second had an open watch.

Big Ear, as the eyes of the ship, was next in line.

"Before the explosion itself, I tried to locate the noise of some ship's propellers," he remembered. "About 100 miles from us. It was definitely not a warship. Probably some fisherman. There were also blue whales singing. Two," he added quickly, as if hoping it would help them somehow.

"I had the depth controls at forty meters."

And so on, they all reported in turn. Then they fell silent for hours.

Only from time to time someone whispered a short sentence with his neighbor. They decided to save batteries and did not turn on their flashlights. Every four full hours they exchanged tapping with their colleagues in compartment four. Then there was another deathly silence.

"I'm suffocating! I'm suffocating!" The younger steward shouted suddenly.

"Calm down! Stay calm!" The captain shouted. "There is still enough air, help will come," he assured them, not believing it himself. He looked at the oxygen measuring device. This one has already passed the green, safe zone for them. And now it was showing the end of the yellow alert state of CO2 concentration in their exhaled air. The red field is the death of all people who breathe this air.

"Put on the apparatus with the CO2 absorber," he said to the steward. And after a while, "everyone put on masks."

It's just an illusory sense of security – apparatus with a carbon dioxide absorber also have their specific suitability for use - short, calculated in hours, not days.

The captain looked at his watch. Phosphorescent hands showed ten o'clock in the morning. It's been twelve hours. He quickly counted: "an hour or two more and the evacuation to the surface should begin. They will die here for sure. And there, too," he thought about it.

"Who's a great swimmer?" He cast the question into the darkness. Hush, no one said anything.

"We need a volunteer to swim underwater down the corridor to get oxygen bottles," he added pleadingly.

He would love to swim himself, but he wouldn't swim very well.

Silence answered him.

"Too cold water, no one will survive the way to the storage room with oxygen devices," the ship's doctor soberly assessed the real chances of such an expedition.

"Yes, you're right, twenty yards one way," the captain agreed, without going back to the subject.

Here and there you could see the faint light of lanterns, the handy ones that everyone had in stock. Some were writing farewell letters on scraps of paper, others were staring at the photos of their loved ones.

We could hear the petty officer praying and someone's soft sobbing, sometimes spasmodic. This did not make others optimistic. Suddenly, the noise of the shot broke into the silence, returning to them repeatedly echoing.

A couple of flashlights came on immediately, searching for the beam of light perpetrators of this sound. The second lieutenant commander was lying in the corner of the room. He shot himself in the mouth with his service pistol. He was the subject of all weapons on the ship. They lost the commander of the torpedo department. For the next fifteen minutes, a buzz of excited voices swept through the entire first compartment. They were on the verge of panic. Only the doctor's balanced voice calmed the situation a little.

"Take it easy, please," he was addressing them firmly. He had a soft, velvety voice, but the confidence in his tone had a calming effect on some.

Others, in the darkness it was hard to tell who, but they couldn't control themselves. The crew was slowly getting scared.

"Silence, that's an order!" The doctor shouted suddenly. It helped, he never raised his voice, so now his scream worked. "I hear something," he added indecisively. He thought he heard some metal knock against the hull.

There was an annoying silence interrupted by the sound of inhalations and exhalations from their air-purifying apparatus.

When they stopped believing that he had really heard something, and an ominous murmur began to rise slowly, suddenly a sound sliced the stale air from top to bottom.

Everyone heard the faint, soft tapping of something not too hard against the metal.

"Radzik, send SOS!" The captain shouted. Sitting on deck with his head down the moody Radzik shot up as if from a catapult.

He quickly realized the knocks were coming from the hatch of their battle conning tower. Instantly, he ran up the rungs.

With the key held down, he tapped three dots, three lines, and then three dots again. He didn't have to wait long for an answer.

There was a steady click of Morse code.

After a while, he began to spell the letters he typed out loud.

"Are you there, anybody?"

"Who is this? They are not ours," it is not known why Big Ear whispered.

"So what, maybe they're Russians."

When the SOMEONE had finished transmitting, there was silence again. But everything in them revived, as if they had swallowed a large goblet of the elixir of life.

Hope flooded their hearts in a broad stream.

They were ready to fight for survival again.

The Captain's firm voice was heard.

"First Officer: prepare the crew for evacuation. Make a list to come to the surface. Wounded in the first place," he ordered. He felt like a ship commander again. He knew what to do and how to save them.

"Third: check the emergency telephone connection and the external socket for receiving external air."

He logically reasoned that if SOMEONE found them in this place and at this depth, they must be adapted to provide help and have a decompression chamber. And maybe even heavy diving equipment. If there are divers, there is also the possibility of blowing air into them.

"Anyone know Russian?" He asked.

"Me, a little," the steward said.

When there was silence, the flashlights were lit. In the glow of the thrown beams of lights, ghostly figures in masks mingled with the cast shadows of their figures, dancing on the sheets and ceiling.

"Anyone have any idea to inform our torpedo tubes about the situation?" He asked further.

"Morse is out, they don't know it," said Radzik.

"Maybe they also heard it?" Big Ear asked.

"I doubt the knocking was soft and THEY are far away."

"Maybe something from the music, some rhythm suggesting rescue," one of the watchmen pointed out correctly.

"But what?" it fell from a distance, "it must be something known and obvious to tap.

"The drummer!" Shouted the 1st Officer, "Play a victory drum for them!"

Klein, a famous amateur musician, took two keys and tapped out the beat of the victory.

After a while, they heard rhythmic thumps: "bum, ram, ram, bum, bum," from the famous movie "Independence Day".

"They got it!" The captain said with satisfaction. He was sitting in his comfortable leather armchair and wondering who had found them, because not their friends from the naval training ship, which always accompanies them in their sea struggles. They would use special explosives to notify them that they are just above them on the surface, rather than knock something on the ship's hull.

Fifteen minutes of annoying silence have passed. Everyone waited in suspense for the rest of the events.

Now they are even ready to come to the surface as they stand. One, two, three, four - they heard the steady, loud hitting of metal on metal.

"It's not Morse," said Radzik.

"These are diver's boots, for sure!" Big Ear said joyfully.

"Hooray! Hooray!" uncontrolled shouts tore silence.

"Calm down!" The First Officer shouted. "Perhaps they are sending something?"

But apart from the sounds of footsteps on the hull, they heard nothing. They waited forever, it seemed minutes turned into hours.

Suddenly there was a distinct scratching noise. There was noise from the loudspeaker of the external emergency communications and crackling.

"This is Captain P." everyone heard a voice clearly with a foreign accent.

# Chapter II

## Storm

I jumped, throwing my hands far in front of me. Maybe I can catch anything - I thought in flight. I hung on the side. I hit it with my whole body, painfully hitting my right hip. I did not think about the pain, the main thing is that the right hand was on the railing. I was thrown horribly to the left, but I didn't let go of this little metal scrap of life. That was the only thing that separated me from the raging element below me.

I looked down, unnecessarily because it would have been better up. The raging cocks of the raging ocean hitting the side fiercely tried to reach me and drag me to the bottom. But they only had enough momentum to whip me again and again with splashes of white water foam carried by the gusts of raging elements. "It's nothing - I'm wet anyway." Through the howling of the wind and the sound of the dull hitting of the waves against the side, I heard the growing roar of

"Poseidon's" machines working at high speed. The captain, turning on the engine all the way back, tries to get away from where he was a moment ago. It was crazy on the part of the Old Man to get so close to this wreckage. He could hit the Quinn's side with his prow at any moment. But there was no other option. Dropping a dinghy or anything else out of the water amounted to committing suicide. It was a slim chance, but the only one we had left. I looked up, waiting for a tilt that would allow me to grab the railing with my other hand. The wreck rocked and it lay down on the other side. I waved my left hand to grab the railing, it shook me hard, but my open hand gripped the metal tube. Now, just the right leg up, swing my whole body over the rail, and in a moment I'm on deck. A quick flick of my hand and I fastened the lifeline latch on some ear next to the railing. That's it, I'm safe for now. I knew the Old Man and the other sailors on the tug were watching me through binoculars, but I grabbed the radio anyway.

I have to tell them, I'm fine.

"I'm on board, safe and sound!" I yell into the radio to shout over the howling of the wind and the sounds of pounding waves on the empty hull of the wreck.

Now it is the turn of the 3rd mechanic. Nobody can help him. Sam has to choose the right moment to jump. He is the only one who decides when it will be relatively safe.

The Poseidon is slowly approaching the side of the Quinn again. Its bow is at the level of the wreckage, to be five or seven meters lower in a moment. The powerful fender on its beak is only an illusion of safety for Edward, kneeling on one knee. When the wave hits the Quinn's side, nothing will protect the bow of the tug and it. The third one is holding with one hand, sticking out next to the seat post, which is attached to the false side of the boat for this time. With his other hand, he squeezes the large eyes of the net wrapped around the fender.

Two more meters - Edward points his fingers to the Old Man, taking one hand from the seatpost for a moment.

The slight movement of the lever and the distance between them decreased to half a meter. So what if there are three meters to the upper deck. Edward needs to wait a while longer.

The Old Man steps back a little and waits for the next wave to take him high. I hear the engine scream in high reverse, and the Poseidon's beak sticks to the Quinn's side. It's high and Edward decides to jump. However, he chose not a very opportune moment. The tug was already going down with the wave, and it hung on the side, holding the lower railing with the fingers of both hands, glued with its whole body to the steel plating. I quickly release my safety line and the three strides between us and the distance between us fall on the deck beside him. One hand movement is enough to secure him to me with my safety line, first wrapping it around the lower railing tube twice. Then I grab the railing with both hands at the same time, lying with my back on the deck with my feet facing the stern of the ship. The left leg, pressed against the transverse reinforcement of the railing, allows me to stay in one place. I can see his right hand move and he pulls up on it, then his left hand, and so on again until his leg rests on the deck. He falls on the deck on the other side of the barrier separating him from the depths of the raging ocean next to him. By raising the thumb of his left hand up, he informs that he is safe. How long did it take? I think. Five, ten seconds? This is the cost of living should something go wrong. The Poseidon threw all the way back and had already moved back to a safe distance from the wreckage. It pivots over port, trying to get close to his bow close enough for them to catch the thin line we fired from the Quinn's bow. The impact of the mountains of water pressing against it lays it down so tightly that it collects the invading waves from the surface on the stern deck as if it were a colander.

After a moment of indecision, he stands up, straightening his slender figure, and falls over to the other side.

"We're going to the bow," I pass to his sternum. We have several dozen meters to walk the deck, which is heavily inclined to the port side, which makes it very difficult for me to go to the bow. I have to grab something stable every now and then and for a moment fasten the safety line latch, which I shortened to one meter from my aching hip. When the wreckage was straightening, I released the latch and walked a few paces on until it was heeled to port again. In such impulses I reached the very bow below the maneuvering deck. And Edward behind me. The metal stairs leading up to the maneuvering deck were badly damaged. It's from a collision with a bulk carrier, I thought, looking at them. Careful, lest my foot fall into a crack, step by step, holding the railings with both hands, I went upstairs to the maneuvering positions. There was a promenade deck above us; on passengers, at least the large ones, the upper deck was for tourists. For the crew, the maneuvering deck was below it, which made our operations extremely difficult. Standing in front of the left-hand windlass, I saw Poseidon approach from the windward direction to the wreckage's bow. I take the orange rescue box, stand next to the bow gate and prepare to shoot.

"Are you ready?" I hear Chief's voice.

"Yes, we are waiting," I reply, looking at the two moving silhouettes of the sailors on board. Hooked with short lines to a nib that had run along the entire aft deck, they balanced their bodies, trying to stay on their feet. I hear a boatswain voice now.

I shoot from the hip with a special rescue target prepared in the port for such an eventuality. I don't have much space for maneuver.

The clearance in the open passenger gate, or rather the lack of closing this gate, is only two meters.

A thin line with a thick knob is flying with the wind on them. It falls to the tugboat's aft deck, somewhere in the middle of it. We can see how the boatswain jumped towards it, covering the distance to the dart in a few steps. He fell to his knees and grabbed its ball.

"There it is, I have it!" He shouts into the microphone.

"Come on!" He calls, pulling it towards him.

Now, Edward and I just have to get it through panama and it'll be okay.

However, this is a big problem for one man. It's good that we were prepared for such a variant of events.

There was already a metal mesh in panama, the eye of which protruded outside the ship, next to the open door.

I attached myself briefly again, very briefly, just enough to allow me to safely lean out through the gate next to the panama. Lying belly down on the deck, leaning halfway out, my left hand holding the side reinforcement, in my right hand I had a piece of metal weight fastened quickly by the Third to the line. With one quick, decisive move I threw it inside the net. Edward was holding the thin end of the dart and to keep it from escaping, he wrapped it in his hand. To make it safer, he knelt on my legs, pinning me to the deck.

"Now it is mine, it will not escape me," I thought, not without satisfaction. I rubbed my eyes with my hand - some insidious wave crashing against the beak flooded me all over. Regardless of this, I quickly stood up, pulling the panama net. I grabbed the rope and began retrieving it on deck. When a second, stylon, much thicker rope tied to a dart passed through panama, I tied its end to a thin nib lying next to the polishes. It was strapped to a shackle, connecting with the end of the anchor chain and suspenders on the port and starboard sides. I reached for my knife at my right side. With a quick movement of his blade, I cut the ties securing the chain against accidental breaking off of the attachment.

"Poseidon, go on!" I called out.

I see the stylon cord slowly disappear behind the Panama, then pull the nib with it. So far, it has been going steadily and without impulses. But when the nib met the resistance of a heavy chain, it tautened and sounded like a string on a double bass. Thick, rusty "Quinn" anchor chain with a great thud it began to slide across the deck, splashing around a lump of paint reflected from the bed. Stirring up clouds of rust-colored dust all around it, it glided across the deck until its beginning disappeared in panama. A few more meters and by the force of his weight he began to fall out of the panama into the water by himself.

We waited a little longer for the weight of the chain, falling into the water from a height of several meters, to break the safety of the harness, which, hitting the sides, fell down. When all the chain in the bow disappeared from my sight, I knew that on the tug they were already attaching its end to the tow.

The Poseidon slowly began to move away from the wreckage's bow, letting more and more thick steel rope behind its stern. The Quinn was on the leash again and obediently followed the Poseidon leading him, his beak facing the wave slowly. So we could focus on what we ended up here for now.

Only yesterday there were three sailors on the wreckage. Everything was normal, they checked in every hour and there were no signs of any surprises. When a storm broke out on this stretch of ocean, what some call the Bermuda Triangle, communication with them ceased. The old man began to worry after three hours.

"What the hell?" He growled as he paced nervously across the bridge.

"Quinn, Quinn!" the Third Officer, who was on watch at the time, called them every now and then.

Silence, nothing, no response. They looked through binoculars, maybe they would see some light signals or whatever. After all, there are so many possibilities to let us know that everything is OK.

But it wasn't - they didn't know what had happened if anything had happened at all.

"Maybe they got drunk and are asleep now," says a Third, but he doesn't really believe it.

The crew of the wreck were raners - motor driver Filip, AB Grzesiek and Maciek 3rd officer (doublet).

None of them abused alcohol, and AB didn't drink it at all.

"If they don't get drunk, what else could be?" asked the petty officer, who, worried about the situation, bothered to bridge.

"They could have poisoned themselves," speculates the Old Man, "this is the most likely scenario," he assures himself.

"You have to find out what is going on there, maybe they need help," he says to them.

And then they heard the cry. I think the Third shouted, but here opinions on the bridge were divided. It could also be AB Grzesiek.

"I can't see them now, but here they are. Devils, devils tell me to kill them!" just that, then there was silence. The old man rushed to the microphone, shouting:

"Quinn, Quinn, what's going on over there? Talk to me!" He repeated it several times.

"Who was he trying to kill?" The boatswain asked.

"Nothing. Silence that lasts until now. The weather is stormy and getting worse, and at night there's nothing to be done, wait until morning," the captain decided.

He settled himself in his captain's chair with the intention of staying there all night. It was early in the morning, and it was already dawn, when sudden, strong gusts of wind came. The wreckage shook as if it had stumbled onto some sandy bottom, and you could clearly see that it slowed down, turning its bow sideways to the wave. This sudden impulse could not withstand the "Poseidon" tow. First he tried to jump out of the water, and when he failed, he tensed and broke off to shoot one end up before plunging back into the ocean. Now the situation has become very dangerous. Leaning sideways to the wave, the Quinn lay on one side and did not get back up, crushed by furious impact of waves crashing hundreds of tons of water against its vulnerable hull. He could sink at any moment, and with him the three reeners from our tug. The captain, having sat all night on the bridge, watched the situation closely. This broken tow forced him to make a risky decision.

"Get Ryszard!" He ordered the boatswain. It was twenty minutes to five. I've done at 4 am I was drinking hot tea and having a light breakfast while sitting in the wardroom when the boatswain came to see me.

"Rysiu, come to the bridge, the Old man is calling you. Tow broke away."

I knew that the tow had broken and that there was still no contact with the reners, so I hadn't gone to bed at all. Swallowing bites of food along the way, I stepped onto the bridge.

"Rysiu, I cannot give you an official order, but you know what the situation looks like. We need to know what's going on there. Will you go?" He asked.

"Who's going with me?" I asked, looking at the bo'sun.

"No, no. The boss can't, someone has to stay here," he explained the situation, seeing my gaze.

"Edward, the 3rd mechanic will go with you."

"Okay, I'm going to get ready."

And so we landed on the wreckage, now sneaking past its main deck toward the entrance to the main dining room. We know a little about the layout of the rooms on the Quinn. When we were standing in Canaveral, Florida, moored to the quay next to the Quinn wreck, we went there to prepare the equipment we needed to jump across the Atlantic. Direction to the Mediterranean Sea, some small port in Egypt - that's where we were supposed to deliver this passenger ship.

It would be in pretty good shape if it weren't for this collision with some huge bulk carrier and would probably still carry passengers to the beautiful ports of South America. A great breach in its bow - from the waterline to the very bridge - and economic reasons meant that its owner decided to sell the ship for scrap, and we had our share of delivering it there.

We watched as all valuable items and devices were dismantled by an American-Canadian company - there were hundreds of people working there. It was already a month before our arrival and with us for another two weeks. I dedicated this time to visiting Florida. First of all, I went with two colleagues to the famous Space Center. John F. Kennedy to watch the shuttles, then a few more attractions, and when they were done dismantling, we hit the road. Everything was going perfectly well until we were behind Bermuda. Then there was silence on the wreck, which, combined with the storm and broken haul, resulted in the fact that now, looking around quickly, we were heading to the upper cabins, where our colleagues had settled. Quinn didn't throw that anymore. "Poseidon" positioned him with his bow to the wave and, flowing forward, tried to survive this emerging hurricane, which, like every year, is born somewhere here, in this region of the ocean. The hurricane's eye was rapidly moving off our course as it headed for the Gulf of Mexico. We went inside the ship.

The huge, empty living room made a depressing impression of the hopelessness of things that were dead and useless. A huge mess she left behind a demolition company, it only heightened this impression.

"Fili!" Edward called out over the radio. They are friends from one city and this probably decided that he volunteered for this escapade. I don't, because it's part of my job and that's what they pay me to wander around in such and other towed objects. Passing the counter where passengers were usually received, we headed up the wide stairs. Three more floors and we were on the highest captain's deck. This is the captain here and its officers had their cabins. Everywhere is empty and silence, broken only by the sounds of a struggling one with the waves of the ship. The cabin in which Filip was located is open, and the door sways once to the left and once clockwise in line with the ship's list. We go there - everything is fine at first glance. No mess, no sign of a fight or anything like that. But Edward notices Filip's phone lying on the floor in the corner.

"What's up? Filip wouldn't have left his phone on the floor. Maybe this is a sign for us?" I thought.

"Here, read, maybe he wrote something on his cell," I say to Edward. I can also, but he'll do it faster, he has the same phone model.

Quick view - nothing is in the notes. He couldn't call anyway - no coverage. It's not a satellite phone, but they had one too. But where is he?

We go to the next cabins. There is a small mess in the engineer's cabin, but that doesn't mean anything - maybe only that he doesn't pay attention to order.

In the cabin of Grzegorz, young AB, satellite telephone is lying on the table.

It is operational - the last call was to us. However, it seems he was shouting these strange words. We can see that in the bedroom, on the door of the cupboard, there is a knife-nailed printout of the e-mail that Grzegorz got in the port.

This is important; the content of the e-mail is so disturbing that we will decide to read it to the captain via radio.

"Not good! Why didn't anyone know about this?" he asks.

His question remains unanswered. This is private correspondence, and Grzegorz did not confide in anyone. Further exploration of the cabins did not bring anything new, which I reported to the old man after another hour of searching.

The short answer was: keep looking.

It's easy to say, but it is a passenger ship, it has several hundred cabins and a dozen different rooms, not counting the entire technical background and the heart of the ship - the engine room with its nooks and crannies. You just can't search it, it could take us all the way and we won't find anything.

Then we directed our steps to the bridge. The huge wheelhouse seemed to convince us like a silent remorse: what are you here for? Everything has died here!

I leaned against the console and gazed out at the tug swaying in the wave.

"Is this the mystery of the Bermuda Triangle again?" I asked Edward.

"Where do you see the triangle here? I don't believe in such nonsense there," he replied to me.

"I don't think so, but there is always a hint of uncertainty in a person, as he reads and listens to these various strange events in this part of the world..."

Suddenly I felt a slight almond scent. I see Edward sensed something too, but I asked:

"You feel that smell?"

"Yes, what is it?"

"This is what roasted almonds smell like," I say to him, looking uncertain. Why are there roasted almonds here? I'm in touch with the captain of the Poseidon, and we're making a quick council on what to do next about these fragrances.

"You'll go and see where the smell comes from later. Just don't hang up," he adds at the end.

We look through the portholes on the port and starboard bridges, surveying the space around the fore deck. We're trying to spot our colleagues.

Suddenly, Edward sees something.

"There, there!" He calls, pointing to the left deck by the quarterdeck.

I look in that direction, but see nothing.

"What did you see?" I ask.

"Nothing. I guess I imagined it," he says, but his gaze shifts to the side. He doesn't want me to see the fear in his eyes. But I guess he got scared of something, jumped too abruptly from the porthole, as if he was afraid that someone would see him.

"Speak!" I said toughly. "Anything can be important," I added.

"But it's impossible, I must have imagined it," still defends itself.

"Talk!" I press on him.

"Two boys, black boys in ship's uniform."

"Are you sure?"

"I am, as long as I don't have any hallucinations," he says, touching his forehead with his hand. "I don't have a fever either."

I immediately associated some facts. But I wasn't sure what I knew and didn't share the news with him.

"Poseidon, Poseidon, this is Quinn," I'm calling the tug. The third looks at me suspiciously.

"You're not going to tell them about it, are you? They won't leave me alone until the end of the contract," he says to me in a pleading voice with a hint of regret that he told me about it.

"No, I won't tell them anything," I reassure him.

"Yes, I can hear you," it's Chief.

"We're going to look for them, we may have a break in communications. There is coverage not everywhere on the ship," I warn him.

"Okay, but go outside every hour and let me know."

"I have a request," I said to Chief not really knowing how to tell him about it.

"Speak, I'm listen."

"I would like to talk to Karol," he is our electrician.

"You can get him."

"He will be soon, what is it? The generator is not working?" he asks.

"No, it's okay, we started it and it's running. There is electricity and so is light."

We had two generators in the corridor. One gave us electricity that powered the lights in the cabins and was cooling our fridge-freezer. The second was an emergency and powered the batteries for Quinn's position lights, because this one, without all aggregates, could not provide us with anything but a place to sleep. We even had our own drinking water.

I hear Karol calling to me:

"Ryszard, what's the deal?"

"I'd like to ask you to check something on the Internet."

"What?"

"Who died in the "Quinn" Collision with a bulk carrier? Can you do it without questions?"

"Okay, as you wish," he replied slightly offended. "Give me an hour."

"Okay, this is what we need to search the nearest places where they can go," I tell him.

"Stay frosty!" he said.

"Rysiu, what's on your mind?" Chief asked.

"It's too early to talk about it now. We'll talk when Karol makes up something. Speak soon," I turned off.

Edward looked at me in surprise. I can see that he is waiting for some clarification. I have to tell him.

"When we were standing in the port, out of curiosity, I entered the site where the "Quinn" collision with the bulk carrier was described. However, I don't remember the details, I only know that none of the passengers was hurt. However, several crew members were killed when the bulk carrier struck the Quinn's bow. They were in cabins next to the waterline. That's all I know."

"You think their ghosts are here?" There was a note of fear in his voice again.

"I don't think anything, I just don't know, but we'll find out soon," I added, "and now we go."

"Come on, let's search their cabins again. There has to be something there to give us a clue."

In cabin of the 3rd mechanic I asked Edward:

"What would you do if you were in danger here? Where would you run, hide and wait for rescue?"

"Shit, I don't know, maybe where I could safely lock myself up?"

"I think so too, but where?"

"Cabins out, rooms and storages as well. Closest to this place, going down the elevator, are the provision stores. The elevators don't work, but the magazines are where they were, and the nearest stairs lead right there."

"Let's go," I say.

We run down the service stairs. It is difficult to recognize here, there are so many of these rooms. We ignore all open doors, paying attention only to closed doors. It's faster that way.

As we walk like this, we shout loudly, crying out over and over now:

"Filip! Grzegorz! Maciek!" but only silence suits us.

To the left is a locked door to some kitchen. There is a straight corridor leading to them from the stairs we came along. They are not closed, only slightly closed. We open it, and there is an empty room, but inside, in the light of the flashlights, we see a second, steel door. Edward comes closer and calls out:

"They are locked with a wedge and a kitchen stool!"

We quickly unlock and open them. At the end of a fairly large room, two figures are sitting leaning against the opposite wall.

"It's Filip and Maciek!" Edward says, shining a flashlight at them.

We quickly run up to them and check if they are alive. They're breathing - that's good, but they're highly poisoned - they're running out of air. I approach Maciek, because he is smaller and weighs little, and Edward to his friend Filip. However, before he threw Maciek on my back like a sack of potatoes, and then he effortlessly lifted his friend and we went up. It was probably the longest staircase in my life - or so I thought then. Once we were on the main deck, where it was light and fresh air, we laid them on the floor. Filip woke up first. He looked at us and whispered unconscious to Edward:

"Watch out for Grzesiek, he wanted to kill us. He's totally crazy."

Then Maciek slowly recovered. The picture of the situation I presented on "Poseidon" was only half a success. Two relatively healthy colleagues were saved. None of us saw Grzesiek again. It is not known what happened to him. He jumped overboard or hid all the way to Egypt? The crew's views on this were as always divided.

Already in the cabin, Maciek and Filip told us how, after unberthing from the quay in Canaveral, Grzesiek locked himself in the cabin and never opened when they knocked on him.

Yesterday at noon, he jumped into their room with a large cleaver, just as they were drinking coffee, shouting:

"Devils, devils want to take me! I have to kill you, they will leave me alone!"

As he walked toward them with that cleaver raised and his eyes blank, they realized it was not a joke and they jumped up the stairs, running downstairs, and he followed them. When he could not open the door in the room where they had locked themselves, he blocked their way back by wedging the bolts. They lost track of time sitting there in total darkness, and as the air began to run out, they lost consciousness as well. Rescue came at the last minute.

After they finished their story, I got through to Poseidon.

"Karol is there?" I asked.

"Yes, waiting with news for you."

"Go on, Karol. What have you learned?"

"All passengers are safe and sound. Eight crew members died, and three were missing, their bodies not found. Two of them are African American boys. Hotel's callboys. I don't know anything about third one."

"All right. Thank you. You helped us a lot," I said.

"In what?"

"You'll find out later," I assure him in a serious voice.

"Maybe you're right they're ghosts," I said to Edward. "Only somehow the middle of the day does not suit me. Since when do ghosts parade in the sun?" I added in an amused tone. "But maybe you're right, I don't know."

After two days, Filip and Maciek were transported to "Poseidon", and I stayed with Edward until the end of the cruise on "Quinn".

After the next two days, I caught both boys scooping our food from the refrigerator. Their story is the irresponsibility, the stupidity of their parents and themselves. Their parents ordered them to go into hiding until they received compensation for their deaths. As they told us, they survived the catastrophe, because where they were supposed to be (that is, in their cabin) they were not there. Back then, they played slot machines in the passenger section, pretending to be the kids of the passengers. After the collision, they hid among them out of fear right up to the Quinn's entrance to the docks, which was easy considering the chaos there was. Grzegorz was considered missing, and among his belongings on "Poseidon" a letter from his wife was found, who informed him that she was leaving him, taking his beloved daughter to another man. Combining these facts with the few empty alcohol bottles found in his drawers and the fact that he could also see black boys, his fate seemed a doomed one.

"And how can you not believe in strange events in the Bermuda Triangle?" I thought, going to sleep. However, something kept me awake. I had a feeling that I was missing something and it was not the smell of roasted almonds at all.

# Chapter III

## Almond Apparition

Our M/V "Quinn" did not belong to the British family of names "Queen Victoria" or any of the "Queen Mary", he was rather their poor relative from the line of South American shipowners who want to earn as much money as possible quickly and easily. Therefore, after the collision, not the fault of Quinn's Captain, but the crew of the bulk carrier, it was patched up in the shipyard and gutted to the limit of anything of any value that could be transferred to another vessel or could be sold.

We had a lot of work with Edward all these days. Contrary to what some might think, we applied diligently and diligently to it, we did what we had to do. So every four hours one of us would come down to the bottom of the ship, to the bow, now with the hotel callboys - Bob or Ken or both. We checked that the patched side was watertight. This part, separated from the rest of the ship, was insulated by shipbuilders, especially for towing, by a steel structure simulating a watertight bulkhead. It consisted in the fact that the entire part of the ship involved in the collision was cut and cleaned by shipbuilders to the bare metal. The torn plating was removed and new sheets were welded in its place. At a distance of about six meters from the side, a steel cage was made surrounding the destroyed part, and one and only door was inserted there with solid bolts. So what when not thought about the fact that to check if there is no water there, you have to open the door. As always, the devil was in the details. Maybe the shipyard workers assumed that no one would open them anyway. What if there was a leak and this makeshift compartment was flooded? Well, by opening it, no one would be able to close the door anymore. The pressure of the water pressing against them would not have allowed it. Therefore, each time I carefully checked whether the steel door was damp and whether there were no trickles of water somewhere. Then I wouldn't open them. And yes, seeing the dry surface of the sheet, I knew there was no water on the other side. After that, I was able to report that everything is OK and that there is no leakage.

However, this was not normal and we were aware of it. Every day we also went to the engine room, all the way to the bilges, to check if it was dry there too. Then watch on the bridge, check the bow anchorage at the bow and so on, every day. The rest is just fun. There were still many attractions on the ship, which one could freely use. One of them was the swimming pool, filled with water by our motor pump, and the bowling pins, which we had played fiercely since Edward had installed the light. The vending machine was not working and had to be adjusted manually, but we didn't mind.

After a few days we felt the smell of roasted almonds again. I noticed the boys behaving strange. They sat in the corner of the living room and did not go anywhere, but looked around anxiously. Edward also got nervous somehow and raised his voice for no reason. One day everyone were sitting in the captain's cabin, in its spacious saloon, when the scent grew particularly intense. I couldn't stand it.

"I'm going to see where it's coming from," I said. "Stay and don't move," I added firmly.

"Don't go Rishard, there are evil spirits," Bob said, and Ken nodded his head in agreement.

"Maybe they're right... What are you going for? There are a few days left, we'll make it to Gibraltar, and the smell will disappear soon," Edward tried to convince me. I didn't listen to them. Equipped with a large flashlight with new batteries, an oxygen cylinder on my back and a mask over my head, I walked down the corridor towards the stern. I was guided by the quite distinct smell of almonds. When I reached a fork in the large dining room, with corridors to the passenger cabins on the left and the entrance to the "entertainment" corridors on the right, I glanced at the floor plan hanging near me. Okay, now to the left and down the stairs to the lower deck. It is from there that the more and more intense smell comes from. It took me about two minutes to go downstairs. It was better here, walking along the corridor I passed a row of glass walls on my left side overlooking the walking deck, and on the right large banquet rooms with a central point in the middle. Now empty and silent.

"The smell was gone. What now?" I thought. I started opening all the doors one by one. In one of them, leading to a corridor, I was hit again by a very intense breath of almond air.

"What is there?" I wondered for a moment, unable to decide whether to go any further.

I tried to remember the layout of the rooms on this level that I had just seen. Yes, there are LUX cabins with portholes along the entire route to the end of the superstructure. I walked in, the door slammed loudly behind me and it went dark. There was no daylight here, and a lit flashlight had to suffice. Shining on the next large, double gates, I read the inscription on them - Screening Room. In the distance, in a shimmering sharp beam of light, I see a fork in the corridor radiating out to both sides. The scent grew stronger. Suddenly, in front of my eyes, about ten meters away, the figure of a woman appeared.

"What the hell?" I thought. She looked somehow strange in the flashlight. I was about to shout at her when she began to glide in a way that I did not understand. Not walk, but somehow steadily move to the other end of the room. Her airy greenish robe rippled over her as she moved forward. I held my breath as she continued to glide forward, her head facing me. Her long blond hair was flowing as if a fan was blowing on it.

Yet the air here was stale, slightly saturated with the scent of almonds. This unnatural movement of hers, green robe and greenish face made thrill passed through my back, and then a shudder and then whole body. Cold sweat was on my forehead, so I automatically wiped it off with my left hand.

What is it or who is it? Questions rang in my head with loud bells.

When she disappeared around the corner, I thought she was waving her hand. A green hand in a wide, airy sleeve.

"Maybe it is some phosphorescent color of the walls that gives such an effect," a thought ran through me. But I dismissed it immediately as ridiculous. The walls of the corridor were not green, but slightly beige.

Releasing my fear, I ran towards her. But I was silent, I did not call anything to her, afraid to disturb the silence that reigned here. Those ten meters aren't that great a distance for her to get away from me. "She couldn't run faster than me," I think to myself. I ran to the fork and looked around. In front of me, the large and wide stairs leading up - were empty. I swept the beam of flashlight around the room.

Nothing, no one can be seen. There is a circular information desk in the center. Now with no maintenance or inseparable computers. "She must have hid there," I thought as I walked in that direction. I looked inside. There is no one here. Then I heard a moan coming from behind my back. Such a long and poignant low moan that turned into a wail. Rapid body rotation backwards. Nothing, no one can be seen.

"Heeelp," I heard clearly, even though it was such a long and moaning scream from a female voice.

"It's some trick, someone is making fun of me!" I couldn't think of anything else. And then I saw her again. She was standing next to the descent. As I was looking at her with the intention of fleeing immediately, her hand slowly lifted upward as if it was having a great deal of difficulty, and nodded encouragingly at me.

"Follow me," she seemed to be saying. Then she airy disappeared into a corridor leading somewhere down. I quickly followed her. All the way down, by several decks.

She was still in front of me, as if it didn't matter how fast I descended. The stairs ended, and she stood at a fork in them, lit by my flashlight. I was sick of this. I turned around with the intention of returning to the top as soon as possible. Then I fearfully saw her standing over me at the top of the stairs, cutting off my way back. I heard a long, moaning screech from her figure, because her bright greenish lips were not moving. The female figure waved over me, and the sounds she made sounded like a plea.

"Heeelp," was hearing again.

Resigned, I turned back to the corridor. She was waiting for me there, only to disappear in a side door. A very strong smell of almonds and something else - like a deadly odor - hit my nostrils. The wide open door encouraged entry. I quickly put the mask on my face and turned on the cylinder valve. There was a sound of inhaled air and a hiss as the air leaked out. It had a calming effect on me. It must be some "cold" store - I thought, looking at the inscriptions on the steel door. I walked slowly inside. A large, empty room with four niches filled with some liquid. "Brine pools!" I realized. This is where they stored fresh fish. I shone my flashlight on their surface. The first and second pools reflected light. In the third, I noticed a dark shadow floating on its surface. I walked closer, lighting it all up. When I realized it was a woman's body, I felt a strong reflex of disgust and fear.

"Run away! Fast!" My consciousness exclaimed. But I regained my composure and looked at the body. She was lying face up, her blond hair rising around her head. She was in a one-piece green suit with a clearly visible ship logo on the front pocket. With her eyes closed, she looked as if she was asleep. Only the light green color of her face made it clear that she was dead. "She must have fallen into the pool during the collision and drowned, but when did her body flow out?" - I was wondering.

I spun on my heel and walked briskly to the exit. Before the stairs I took off my mask and I started running. When I reached the fork in the corridors, something made me look round. I stopped and I turned my head. She was standing behind me smiling and holding hands in front of me as if in thanks. Surprisingly! The face and hands were no longer green. It was too much for me. I sprinted towards the upper deck. I ran until the very end. When I burst into the captain's lounge, everyone knew something was wrong.

Edward then said to me:

"You fell as if someone was chasing you. Red on face from effort and with trembling hands. You couldn't utter a single logical word. You mumbled something about some apparition and repeated two words over and over: 'I found her, I found her'.

'Who?' I asked then. 'Almond Apparition.' You answered us.

When we took your oxygen cylinder off and you gulped down all Coke, you said in a calm voice: 'There is the ninth victim of a collision. It is in the fish warehouse in the pool with brine'."

Since then, the smell of roasted almonds has not appeared anymore. We arrived at Gibraltar. There both callboys went ashore, assisted by the police, and the appropriate services took the woman's body. It is not known yet who it is. But they are to let us know when they identify her. To this day, the question bothers me - where does this almond smell come from? Nobody could give me a meaningful one and a convincing answer.

But is it important? It is important that the "Almond Apparition" will have a funeral and that her soul will be at peace. I did not tell anyone about her, what for? Nobody would believe me anyway. Sometime after this event, I wasn't quite sure if I had dreamed it up sometimes.

I explained it to myself with the "sixth sense". Since then, my sixth sense has spoken whenever I am in danger.

For Grzegorz, the company sent Jarek to "Poseidon", who was waiting for us there for three days, hanging out in a hotel in Gibraltar.

"Guys, it was a holiday weekend! I was walking around and explored this huge rock. I even climbed the cable car to the top to feed the monkey," he boasted. "But then I ran out of money and I was alone at the nearby bars, sipping cold English beer," he finished in a less cheerful tone.

I was glad because Jarek was a bit younger than me, but I had quite good contact with him. Like me, he was a company diver with a professional diver diploma and we could talk for a long time about our passion for conquest the deep sea. The "Poseidon" with the "Quinn" in the tow slipped unhindered between the charming Mediterranean islands, safely reaching its destination port. Now we quickly passed our "passenger" and without the usual delay, without entering the port, we headed towards Ceuta, where we were to bunker fuel for the jump to Reykjavik. It took us all the way back to discuss the events on the Quinn.

Those who were not there had the most to say. As usual in such cases, the stories have grown into a good horror movie with the great unknown in the background. Even though they wanted me to tell them how I ended up in the brine pool and where the almond smell came from, I never told them about the Almond Apparition. I had a feeling this was what she wanted. From Algaciras, Spain, near Gibraltar, we took a large broken fishing factory to tow, and then we headed to Iceland and their home port - Reykjavik. Almost all of its crew sat on the ship. Due to lack of work, having stocked up on various kinds of alcohol, they drank to Iceland itself. This time I didn't land on it, and thank the Old Man for not giving me there. The enormous stench and dirt that prevailed there could scare any reasonably clean person. How did they live there? This was a question that I didn't know I'd visit, but it was definitely not pleasant. Keep at the breakfast, two days before Iceland, announced new news in the mess.

"We have a new job. From Iceland, we're going to Canada high north, there's Naomi Harbor, where two merchant ships are waiting for us. We have to haul them to Egypt for scrap. Because the road to Egypt will take us some time, in Canada, everyone who hired as a crew member three months ago are finishing their contract and returning to the country."

I was eligible for this return because I had less than a month of the contract left. I was pleased - time passed quickly, and the waters in which we moved were familiar and predictable, not like the African ports and their coastal waters. Although - as time has shown - it was not quite so, and fate did not spare us further surprises.

# Chapter IV

## Whale singing

Suddenly I fell into an invisible water current, it's some kind of underwater river. Its speed and strength surprised me completely. Somewhere here, I knew, the Labrador Stream was connected to the North Atlantic Gulf Stream.

It was pulling me down quickly. I turned like a wheel, and the current pushed me straight towards the submarine lying on the bottom. Despite the fact that I was swinging my legs with large fins with all my strength, I still couldn't control the situation.

"When will they finally realize it's not a pool race up there and they'll hold my safety line?!" I thought, spreading my hands like the wings of an airplane.

One thing I feared the most: the impact in an uncontrolled manner against any dangerous protrusion on the ship's hull. I twisted a few more times on my own axis as the lifeline began to hold me down. Another four or five meters and I would be above the immense, inert body of the ship. Were it not for this hump on its hull, it would resemble one of the blue whales that have accompanied us for some time. It is because of them that I am here. Slowly, held by a line attached to a pontoon floating on the surface, I approached its bow. I pressed my feet against its steel cover, but the current broke me and my head I moved forward like a dead herring towards its combat conning tower. I gave in to it only controlling direction so as not to miss this giant a black ulcer growing out of the middle part hull. Stretching out my arms forward, I cushioned hitting its vertical wall, and still smacking mine lead clamps in its surface. A second later I caught a metal ladder climbing on the very top. The current pressed me against his steel plating. It was well. I spread my feet like a frog, sliding the fins to the side. Now I could slowly shifting with my hands and feet, move towards his top edge. When I was at the top, not releasing the last rung of the ladder, I pushed myself in its enormous depths. I stood on the steel body of closed hatch. Just the head was sticking out beyond the conning tower.

"Shit," I thought, "it was supposed to be just a relaxing practice dive, not an encounter with this shipwreck."

I look down at the hatch, but it's locked. Now I can look around freely; the water current flows around the conning tower, giving me the opportunity to stand freely on its deck. I no longer have to fight an underwater river trying to carry me deeper into the ocean. I look at the bow of the ship, then at its stern. I can't see anything special, maybe just that it is leaning slightly to the port side and with a large aft trim. "It probably struck his beak to the bottom," I think. "But I won't go there to check. There is no need. It's not very safe here. I must go back now."

I bent over the hatch to see if is it firmly locked. It was. Out of curiosity, I banged the metal hilt of my knife against its bolts a couple of times, checking that they would not move. They hadn't moved and were still firmly in place.

What was my confused surprise with horror when I heard a knock coming from inside it. Loud and clear tapping. S. O. S. - three dots, three lines, three dots - someone was sending from the center of the fuselage.

I wanted to pinch myself, but couldn't.

In rubber insulated gloves, this is rather impossible. No, it's not an illusion, the sound in the water is perfect. I couldn't be wrong.

"What now?" I overwhelmed myself and, very nervous, tapped Morse: "are you there, anybody?" I made an obvious mistake, but there was no time to correct it.

I didn't wait long for an answer.

"...WE LIVE! HELP!" A moment of break.

"...OXYGEN CAN LAST US FOR ONE, TWO HOURS!" I spelled the tapped letters.

I went numb, I was expecting everything except that there was someone alive. Some kind of miracle?

"What the hell? How did they get here? How long are they at the bottom?"

These and other questions quickly flashed through my mind.

"We rush to your rescue. Wait!" I tapped a message with Morse for them.

Throwing off my leaden belt, I burst onto the surface in an emergency. I left right next to the pontoon.

They pulled me inside quickly. Quickly taking off the mask, I threw in their direction:

"To the decompression chamber! Hurry!"

The pontoon, raising its bow up, was running with the force of its two engines towards the Poseidon.

"Get the chamber ready. Hurry!" The boatswain shouted into the radio.

On the way to the tug, they took the equipment off me and the suit. After half a minute I was at the side, and after ten seconds I was in the chamber. The hiss of air made me realize that this time I could make it.

Thirty-four meters - that's what my diving watch showed. This depth was at the ship and they served me the same pressure in the chamber. Now I was at the same depth, but locked inside this steel monster. I was in it sooner than the Old Man got down from the bridge.

Now he was standing by the porthole of the chamber, microphone in hand, shouting:

"Are you crazy?! You don't like your life?! What the hell is this? Why are you not up to the standards?"

"I couldn't, Captain," I said finally after he stopped yelling at me. "There's a submarine over there. There are living people there. They only have oxygen for one or two hours. They need immediate help."

He looked at me, sticking his nose to the window of the chamber porthole, not quite believing that I was normal and not raving about decompression sickness.

"I don't know from where, what or how, but they tapped Morse code for me from inside this submarine," I'm trying to convince him by speaking calmly and clearly.

"Look at me," I hear his nervous voice with a hint of uncertainty. "How many fingers do you see?"

"Three."

"And now?"

"Seven."

"Okay, what else?" Asks stupidly frant, as if what I have said so far was not enough for him.

"Nothing, the rest is not my business," I said, "for the next half hour of sitting here," I add.

This is how long it takes to safely exit the decompression chamber.

The captain looked at me again.

"Ryszard, are you sure? You know what will happen if you get it wrong?!"

"Captain, I certainly wasn't seeing things," I assure, looking at him.

I sit on the couch and talk to him on the extension phone, trying to convince him. "They are there and they need help," I add. "Immediately."

"Okay, I'm going to notify the emergency services. Just don't get out of here sooner," he says unnecessarily.

Even if I wanted to, it is impossible to get out from the inside - except in an emergency.

At the Canadian Rapid Reaction Force Base at the Maritime Rescue Center a calm but firm voice came from the red speakers, speaking English with a Slavic accent.

"Mayday, Mayday. This is Captain P. from the Polish Ocean Tug "Poseidon". An unidentified submarine has crashed and calls help. I give its and my position."

"How did it get there?" Asked the captain of Sanok, who was sitting next to the computer technician, responsible for the coordination of activities and liaison with those calling for help.

"How did he find them?" Asks in a surprised voice a question that so far no one can answer.

The duty officer, Commander Nills Ganasa, immediately enters the data into the computer and presses the red alarm button for the Underwater Rescue Service subordinate to him.

He is sitting in a large, spacious room full of computers and command posts facing the wall with huge integrated screens with their computers. All stands of people working there face the front wall in semicircular rows like in some cinema, each of them has its own area and scope of activity. The satellites on the wall screens show the view of the globe as on a large geographical map. Below is a series of rapidly changing numbers and letters showing individual locations, weather, temperature, and other important data needed to correctly assess the situation in the region.

After entering the data into the satellite, which covers the area with the position given by the tugboat, the central screen shows a large fragment of Greenland with Cape Farewall. Its scale changes rapidly and after a while, the screens show an anchored tug calling for help for a submarine. You can see a dark oblong object in the water from the port side nearby.

"Depth: 41 meters," reports the operating technician.

"Our fleet exercises are taking place near them," says the commander of the Naval Aviation Group. He immediately connects with the commander of the flagship missile destroyer and presents him with the situation.

The signal from the Poseidon was also received there.

"We have had no communication for fourteen hours with our submarine involved in this exercise," a disturbing thought flies through the mind of Commander Peter Wilson as he receives a report on a distress signal.

"Send a recon plane immediately, have it identify the ship lying on the bottom!" his order is given to the destroyer commander. After three minutes, an anti-submarine plane took off from the Canadian Air Regiment military base closest to the CONDOR area. Its task is to identify the submarine and then try to establish communication with it.

Rescuers from a special Sub-marine Parachute Assistance Group (SPAG) are on duty in a small building located nearby, close to the helicopter landing area. The alarm signal distracts them from their mundane activities.

Everyone runs to the central check-in room. They have five minutes to read and assess the situation and select the appropriate equipment for the action.

"An unidentified submarine has crashed," reports the commander, officer in charge of the SPAG Group. "It is 40 meters under water, next to the Cape Farewell islet, the water temperature is about four degrees. Good visibility, water current up to 9 knots. They are running out of oxygen, they are already in emergency CO2 absorbers. At the scene of the accident, the Polish rescue tug is trying to supply them with air and establish telephone communication via emergency lines.

They have a decompression chamber and an underwater camera, but they do not have any specialized equipment that would enable the crew to safely evacuate the ship.

Their diver is already in the water and is trying to connect them with hoses forcing air inside the ship. That's all we have for now," he shows them the situation.

"To the cars, start in twelve minutes," he gives the command. "Arrival time in about four hours," he adds and moves away from the large map with the place of their drop marked.

Everyone ran outside the building to the hangar for equipment, where cars were waiting for them to take them to the nearby airport. In half an hour they were in the air.

I lay down on the couch and thought about how I got here. We were already sailing for the second week, thrown across the endless waters of the ocean to the distant land of singing whales. It was weird - after all, we were not a research vessel, but an ocean-going tug on the way to the port, where two broken and rusty ships were waiting for us, about to end their lives on one of the beaches in Egypt, where they would turn them into the proverbial "razor blades".

The singing of whales - blue whales - was with us on the second day. The loneliness of these large mammals in their annual journey through the cold waters of the ocean here can be compared to the loneliness of a matros traversing this reservoir, although for a completely different purpose. We sail quite close to the shore to stay away from the designated zone reserved for Canadian Navy exercises. Inland view covered here and there with a cold rug of icy snow, it recalled in my mind the cheerful crackling of the fire in the fireplace. It's like a contrast, although I wasn't cold at all. It was a beautiful sunny day. I went outside dressed warm in my Norwegian jacket and padded pants. Outside, the temperature was above zero - six or eight degrees, a light wind and a cloudless sky encouraged relaxation and admiring the local views. I was just watching a beautiful wild panorama of uninhabited areas of land covered with clumps of icy snow, when my attention was caught by an otherwise strange sight. Two blue whales came very close to the ship and majestically, zigzagging, crossed its course, turning from left to right on our bow. I turned to the companionway, sticking my head into the engine room hatch, where the fitter was messing with something in his workshop.

"Bronek!" I screamed deeper into the engine room.

After a while, Bronek's head appeared, shining with a bald head.

"What?" I guessed more than I heard what he was saying to me. Though he tried to shout over the sound of the tug's machinery working, I couldn't hear much.

"Come upstairs," I shouted, gesturing with my hand to leave.

He took the headphones off his head and started up the ladder.

"What happened?" He asked, waving his hands coldly because he was dressed as if it was the middle of a hot summer outside. No wonder - the temperature in his place was over forty degrees there.

"We have company. Look over there."

Two beautiful black tail fins were just disappearing into the depths of the ocean, waving rhythmically at us as if they wanted to tell us something.

"Go get dressed and come right away, there is something strange in their behavior. And bring your camera, we'll take some pictures. I'm going to the bow, it will be better to see from there," I shouted to him.

Bronek liked the view, so without further ado he disappeared inside the quarterdeck. After two or three minutes, the two whales reappeared in front of the bow.

They crossed our course as they swam side by side as if to stop us.

"It's weird," I muttered to myself.

"What are they doing? Bronek asked and started slamming the shutter of his Canon. I looked up at the bridge. You could see the Third, leaning his elbows on the porthole, looking through binoculars at the whale.

"We're about to hit them, what's going on?" Bronek asked with a slightly nervous voice.

"I don't know, but I'm going upstairs," I can see that the Third called the captain, whose silhouette just appeared to me.

"Ryszard, how long have you been watching them?" The captain asked as I stepped onto the bridge.

"About half an hour."

"What's wrong with them?"

Suddenly, one of them, with a sharp turn - if you can talk about something like that with his huge body weight - turned right onto our side and hit it with his side, as if he wanted to push us off course. We were a bit shaken. The captain took the telephone receiver off the console and pressed the key connected to the engine room.

"We're stopping," he said to the mechanic. "Just stop the engine slowly."

Others felt the slight shock, too, as the phone on the bridge rang. The old man grabbed both handles of the engine room grips and put them in the STOP position. After a while, you could hear the engine slowing down, so that after a minute there was silence on the ship.

"Less than a mile to land," said Third, looking at the on-board computer screen.

The whales made a circle and stopped in front of our beak as if they were watching us stand in a drift. Several figures of sailors appeared on the tank, and, concerned about the shock, they went out on the deck to see what we had hit. But they saw nothing but the enormous bodies of two blue whales gliding towards us.

"They will ram us," Bronek mentioned, looking through the binoculars at them.

"Are they attacking us?" I think aloud, looking at the Captain.

"They can't do anything to us, they'll do themselves any harm," you can hear the quiet voice of the Old Man. "But by the way, what do these whales want from us?"

"They're two hundred yards from the bow," he tells us Third."

They approach slowly, but all the time their ridges protrude above the surface of the water. About a hundred yards ahead of us, they suddenly separate, moving in a semicircle from us in order to make a loop - one from our port and one from our starboard. After a while they stuck to us, taking us into their oppression. Just like they do when they take their little offspring among themselves, either to protect them from the orcs, or to direct them to swim a certain direction. The strong blows of their tails suggest that they really intend to do so.

I followed the captain on board. Leaning overboard, I admire their enormous bodies, almost as big as our "Poseidon". The tug's bow slowly moves towards the shore.

"I haven't seen anything like that!" exclaims Bronek, not taking the camera from his eye to press the shutter button again and again.

"And I have not even heard of something like a whale sticking to the side of a ship," Jarek tells us with an excited voice.

"He stuck it on maybe not, but I once read on the Internet that he attacked a small boat that swam too close to a small whale, but it was black, that is, the hull was black, so it could be mistaken for killer whale," explains the Chief, engineer, elbows leaning against the ship's side staring at the back of the whale. The captain, leaning overboard, grabs the radio:

"Slowly go forward," he commands the Third.

"Ster midships."

"You can't see anything there, nothing but bare rocks," he continues, looking straight ahead.

The whales no longer wave their tails as if they are pleased with the direction we are now going.

"Give the depth," the captain says to the Third.

"Four cables to the shore, one thousand two hundred meters under the keel."

We look surprised at this unusual sight.

"It's some magic! Or maybe they are sick and their instincts are malfunctioning?" Chief wonders.

"Two of them immediately suffer from the same disease and both have the same loss of instinct? No it is not possible," the 2nd engineer is opposed.

"I read somewhere that the dolphins saved a drowning child in this way. Keeping them afloat," Jarek interrupts the conversation, looking at the whale's enormous breathing spikes that look like a tractor tube.

"Yes, yes, but this is what they did to their newborn dolphins so that they could breathe, and sometimes they have to do that too," the 2nd mechanic explains his thought.

"Three hundred meters to the shore, sixty meters deep," you can hear the voice of a Third.

"Machines stop," commands the Old Man.

"Bo'sun at anchor," he adds, turning to Józwa.

We are slowly approaching the shore with our own impetus. Suddenly two whales, singing in high tones their song, at the same time they broke away from us and wagging their tails, they passed us a little. Being in front of the bow they dived, exposing their giant tail fins for the moment.

With a loud splash, they plunged into the water, disappearing from our sight. Having swam a bit more, we drifted.

"Left to the water, four shackles on the elevator," the captain gives the command to the boatswain.

The rumble of the anchor brings everyone back to speech. So far we have been silent, as if we were afraid to scare these beautiful giants. The largest animals in the world do not know that they are - or maybe they do, because they have enemies - humans and orcs that hunt them. Orcs, hunting in a herd, are also dangerous for them. Rarely do they dare to attack them directly, they mostly kill young whales, first separating them from their mother.

Poseidon is slowly moving its bow into the wind.

"Four shackles anchor on the elevator," hear the boatswain.

"Strong," the captain replies.

"And what now?" asks the Third Officer, "Where are they?" He wonders, looking through the binoculars.

They have not disappeared. On the port side, a hundred yards beyond our stern, a geyser of water gushed out. It was the whale that put its huge head above the surface of the water and, glaring at us with its great eye, looked at us, only to slowly plunge back into the ocean in a moment. After a while he repeated the maneuver again. Again. And once more.

"Is it the same or do they take turns?" I wonder, looking at their swimming performances. "But isn't that some way of communicating with us?" I wonder aloud as I turn to the captain.

"They want to tell us something?" the Old Man wonders, but not only he, everyone is discussing what it can mean.

"I bet it's some kind of fun. But we will not dive after them," says the 2nd mechanic. "Because I think they want it," he notes.

"What are you saying, fun? They want to tell us something clearly, just what?"

"Anyone have an idea?" The captain asked.

Nobody said anything.

"Depth: forty-eight meters," reports Third from Bridge.

"I wish we had sonar," said the boatswain.

"What do you need sonar for?"

"Maybe a wreck is sunk here?"

"Maybe with gold and with pirates?" the second mechanic laughed.

But that's a smart thought - it dawned in my head.

"Captain," I say, "maybe there is something at the bottom here and they want to tell us about it?"

"But what could be here?" The Old Man wondered.

"Third, are there any markings on the map?"

"No, there's nothing. Clean, smooth, rocky, then quite steep," answered the Third.

"Hmm!... All right, we'll do some routine exercises. You will go underwater with Jarek to check the hull, rudder and propeller. And by the way, take a look around. But what about whales?" He wonders for a moment, gazing at the water around the ship.

"It is too shallow here for them and therefore very dangerous," I add, glad that I will dive, but I have to dispel his doubts. "They swam into deep water, for sure."

"They swam away?" asks the Third.

The third examines the water surface around the ship through binoculars.

"How's going?" The captain urges him.

"Yes, you can't see anything."

"Maybe they don't remember how much the blue whale can withstand under water, probably an hour," I think to myself.

But from Discovery, I know they're completely harmless to humans, so why not try scuba diving in the cold waters of the North Ocean?

"Diving team, let's start," Jarek calls, as pleased as me. Nothing like a change from the monotonous sailing of the ocean.

We check equipment, cylinders, a decompression chamber, suits and everything that belongs to us. About forty meters to the bottom. The water is fabulously clean, but also fabulously cold. It is going to be interesting, I have never dived in these waters before, so I don't know what to focus on. AB and the boatswain have already left the pontoon and are preparing the underwater camera, checking the vision on the monitor in the diving room.

"All right!" A diving man calls over the intercom. At this time, I wear white tight pants and a sheep wool sweater, and a balaclava over my head. I put on a rubberized insulated suit, fasten my helmet with a stiff collar, pull a rubber insulated hat over it, then put on my big blue mask and buckle my personal weighted lead belt. Just my inseparable fins and I'm ready. I am completely isolated from the water, there is none a piece of my body that would come into contact with the cold water of the ocean. Damn, what about the safety line? - I struggle with her poorly clarified scroll. It's bad without it, and even worse with it. It is not always helpful, and sometimes it can be disturbing or even dangerous. It would get tangled up in some goddamn trouble.

"There are strong underwater currents here," says the Third, who came down from the bridge to us. "You have to be careful with them. They can be up to nine knots by location."

"For the time being I am not attaching myself," I say to Jarek, who, standing next to me, is just finishing getting dressed.

As the second diver he will protect me. My camera is already in the water. They are two yellow floats, in the middle of which there is a large specialized camera for underwater photos. It does not have its own drive, so you have to work a bit with it when shooting underwater. Now it's swimming calmly, held by the bridle by the boatswain leaning out of the pontoon. I go down the dive ladder to the water. A slight chill engulfs my hands, wearing warm rubber gloves. The rest of the body is well insulated from the cold water because I felt nothing. After a while I am at the pontoon and hold the camera with both hands. I begin to descend lower and lower, looking around curiously. The water is transparent and the bottom is clearly visible, despite the fact that below me is twenty meters. Directing the "searchlight" eye - this is what we call our underwater trinket - at the hull of the tugboat, I slowly swim along its side. I wonder if the hitting the whale's side left any trace. Their skin is hard and rough, but I could see nothing on the hull except some scratches that might have been something else entirely.

.Having reached the rudder and propeller, I find that there is nothing interesting to see there. Now I look at the underwater horizons, I think, plunging below the hull. I feel a slight gust of current pulling me towards the open ocean. I surrender to it and descend ten meters lower.

Rocky bottom, covered with some layer of silt or sludge. You can see fish flitting here and there. Following them with my eyes, I simultaneously direct the camera's eye there, then I turn towards the depth, where the bottom gently slanting downwards.

Suddenly, in the distance, a black, longitudinal stain appeared to me. Several dozen meters from me, I can see something in the vibrating light pushed by the water current. I film it with the camera for a while so they can get a good look at it upstairs. I decided to check what it is, but without the unnecessary ballast that a searchlight would become for me, so I slowly rise to the surface. The pontoon is already approaching me. "Take it" - I show them with my hand at the camera. Having grabbed the round sleeve of the pontoon, I grab the end of the lifeline and attach it to my belt. I show Jarek my thumb up and, bending to the bottom, I dive quickly into the water. They already know about the mysterious object lying nearby at the bottom. They were instructed by the captain to secure me very carefully. I swim towards the dark shape, plunging into an ever stronger stream of an underwater river. I don't know that yet, but I am concerned about whether it is sometimes the notorious Labrador Stream or the Gulf Stream of the North Ocean. I am swimming about two meters above the bottom, constantly increasing in depth.

What is this dark spot, maybe it's blue whale lying at the bottom?

Goes through my head. Probably dead, or else he would have had to come to the surface a long time ago to get some air. Was this what they wanted to show to his kin? - I think quickly, approaching this mysterious and intriguing spot.

It's getting darker and darker, but I can already see that it's definitely not a whale. The hump on its elongated body excludes this possibility. It's a wreck! It's dawning on me. Submarine wreck. What's he doing here? - I wonder. It's shallow here and not marked on the map. Maybe it's some missing submarine. So much has been heard about their mysterious and unexpected disappearances.

I quickly swim closer. As I swim to it, I don't see anything special. But I don't know anything about submarines. I wonder why it's not overgrown with shells? I think in my mind.

I look up and around myself. Apart from the dark spot of the hull of our pontoon, nothing else can be seen on the surface of the water. Whales too. I am still several dozen meters away from the wreckage. I look at my watch: I have twenty minutes. I can be with the ship so much. The rest is time spent safely emerging from this more than thirty-meter depth. My safety line goes up in a semicircle.

I closed my eyes...

"Are you sleeping?" I heard a tapping on the chamber, and then the voice of a Third, who came to check if everything was OK.

"No, I'm not asleep anymore. I can't wait to leave," I tell him.

"I'm going to Jarek, he will go under the water," he tells me. "I'll be back to you in a moment."

"Okay, go, I'm not going anywhere." I knew the captain was very busy alerting the relevant emergency services to find a sunken submarine with a crew inside. I also know that he has issued appropriate orders to take all possible measures to save the crew there. And we had such opportunities, we just need to take advantage of them. Meanwhile, I have to stand here and wait for all the nitrogen to come out from my blood and I can safely leave the chamber. But they, on the ship, didn't have that time, so I risked an accelerated return to the surface. Now our entire crew is getting ready to help them. Probably Jarek is already in the water and is looking for a possibility of connecting an oxygen hose to their interior. We have the option, but we don't know if they have a proper link to it, and if it isn't sometimes in a sunken compartment. Because some part of the ship had been flooded, I had no doubts. Otherwise, they would have given some signal to their command. I look at my watch - ten more minutes. What the hell is this time so slow?

A third comes up to me, takes the microphone and says:

"Ryszard, Jarek goes down in a diving suit. He asks where the sound from the ship was coming from."

"I was standing in the center of the battle conning tower, knocking on its hatch. My lead belt is there. Get him out. Do you already know something?" I ask.

"No, nothing specific. The Old Man alerted all possible emergency services. Hope you are right about the knocks inside of it?"

"I'm not wrong. What are you going to do?"

"Look for opportunities to provide them with oxygen," this is a priority.

"I have to go, I'll be here in ten minutes," he says, disappearing from the porthole.

Shit, and I'm not there right now - I'm nervous about this inactivity. Why didn't they fire a rescue buoy? - I wonder. They didn't even have to do it themselves. It should automatically break free from the ship and float to the surface, sending a signal. They must be equipped with more than one such rescue buoy with a satellite signal showing their position. I wonder about the cause of their radio silence and other emergency notification options for their submarine's disaster. What about the Escape Pod for the crew? They probably don't have it or it has been destroyed.

I haven't seen the whole ship, maybe it has some external mechanical damage, like a torpedo hit or an explosion inside, maybe a torpedo or something damaged the ship enough to prevent them from successfully calling for help.

These are the thoughts that bother me while lying on the couch and staring at the hands of the decompression clock that slowly measures the time to open the chamber door.

# Chapter V

# Hope

The Third broke me out of my thoughts.

"We open it," I heard his voice, and then the click of bolts in the round door of the chamber. The air pressure was even so I didn't hear any hiss.

I'm going out; it's time for me to join the rescue operation again. I took my blood pressure, did a few squats, push-ups, and quick breaths and exhales checking that I'm okay. We don't have a doctor, so I have to find out if I'm healthy and I'm fine. It didn't hurt, so I changed quickly and, assisted by the third officer, I went on deck, and from there to the diving room. I look at the monitor and see Jarek in the water in a diver's suit, looking for an emergency air intake that is located somewhere beside their combat conning tower. The rigidly mounted camera shows us a large fragment of the submarine. We want to connect a compressed air hose to its hull. Then just forcing the air inside and waiting for a signal from the crew. The captain is calling from the bridge with the information:

"The submarine belongs to the Royal Canadian Navy and has participated in exercises in these sea areas. They sent us its photo and technical drawing with the layout of rooms, plan of watertight bulkheads and emergency exits. They marked the places where links for air and underwater telephone are."

The parachute team will be there in four to six hours. Until then, our tug is an auxiliary unit and is responsible for establishing communication with the submarine using the submersible telephone and for supplying them with air. A Canadian Navy plane flew overhead. They did circles for fifteen minutes and took off. Jarek has already found the right link to give them compressed air. It is not yet known how they will be distributed around the ship and whether it will be useful to the crew waiting to be evacuated. He also found an emergency escape hatch on the starboard side next to the conning tower, allowing the attachment of an emergency bell or a rescue vehicle to it. Unfortunately, "Poseidon" did not have any specialized equipment with which it could safely evacuate the crew from the sunken submarine. The captain was also asked to try to board the ship in order to check the general situation, the pressure there and whether people should not be evacuated immediately. It was known that none of the submarine's crew might not survive the pressure changes that may occur when rescuing them from this depth. What about the water temperature?

I remembered the events of the Peruvian submarine "PACOCHA", which sank in 1988, and its crew quite efficiently and quickly was evacuated to the merchant ship accompanying rescuers, on which, unfortunately, there were no decompression chambers. The lack of such a chamber meant that the initial success of the rescue operation turned into a great tragedy.

The evacuated seamen were paralyzed as a result of decompression sickness, and some died of air jams, although they were under a pressure of about four bars.

If a sunken ship stays on the seabed for a long time and is partially flooded, and its crew is under a pressure of 4 bar, as in that case, the decompression time is approximately 30 hours. But it is not so clear cut. Each of the crew members in different compartments of a sunken submarine may be under different pressure, and therefore must undergo different decompression. Each crew member of a damaged submarine lying on the seabed, regardless of whether it is injured or not, will not survive the pressure changes that may accompany its rescue, and this is the biggest logistical problem that occurs during the emergency evacuation of people from a sunken submarine.

Jarek quickly connected the telephone cable to the external emergency communications. There was silence in the dive room. Everyone was waiting for the effect with anxiety. Crackling and hum echoed from the intercom speaker.

"None of this - no communication," said the Third Officer on the line.

Captain P. picked up the microphone.

"This is Captain P. from the tugboat of the Polish Ship Rescue," he said.

Suddenly amidst the noises and crackles they heard quite clearly:

"This is Captain of SSK-264, Commander Harry Montery, reporting the ship's emergency. Mayday! Mayday! We need air immediately! We are..."

The voice was gone. We see on the monitor screen how Jarek is messing with the link there.

"It will get better soon," we hear his voice.

"I haven't completely vented the socket yet," he explains in a thin, squeaky voice, the effect of the pressure changing the timbre of his voice.

"...18 of us, and the second group of crew in the bow - thirty-eight people," it can be heard quite clearly.

"Switch to the rescue channel," orders the Third.

"We hear you well, Commander," the Old Man replies. "We'll connect the air in five minutes. Help on the way. Canadian and American emergency services alerted, rush to your rescue."

Now all warships and rescue services hear the conversation between them.

"Is the emergency hatch in your compartment in working order?" asks Captain P.

"Yes, checked, it is operational, but the rooms with evacuation equipment are flooded and we do not have access to it. We lack oxygen apparatuses, thermal suits. Everything," ends the counting shortly.

"Which compartment is the rest of the crew in?"

"Fourth bow compartment. 38 people from the crew. There was an explosion in the stern of the ship and a fire in the engine room. We have no communication with them. Maybe someone survived there."

Now the commander of the rescue operation, Commander Nills Ganasa of the Canadian Navy, joins the conversation.

While they are lively exchanging information, I, with the help of the boatswain and AB, re-dressed in my personal scuba suit.

As I finished dressing and only had the mask collar left to put on, the captain entered the dive room, addressing the entire crew gathered in that small dive room.

"I have received a request from the Royal Canadian Navy to consider entering the ship. According to their assessment, it can be entered through the emergency hatch.

After establishing communication with the ship's crew, they can open and close the hatch even if no systems on the ship are working. Provided that it is not mechanically damaged."

"What about the pressure?" I ask. "Inside the escape hatch, first equalize the pressure to the level outside the ship, and then, when I will inside, push the water out of there. This is a very dangerous operation, and I can get stuck there if they don't do it fast enough."

"They claim that it is possible with compressed air, which, regardless of other factors, is permanently associated with securing the escape hatch."

"Well. If necessary, I will go. But why should I go there?"

"According to the information obtained from the crew, seventeen of them are in the command post in the middle compartment of the ship. There is not a single oxygen apparatus there. They only have apparatus to purification of the air from carbon dioxide, and they are not suitable for immersion in water."

"I know that much," I think to myself.

"Twenty-eight breathing apparatus are in the storage near their compartment, but the road to them is flooded. You have to provide them with two apparatus, and they will take out the rest themselves."

"They won't pull out, the water is too cold," I think about the four steps water has overboard. "What's the pressure there?" I ask the captain.

"No one knows, it's a flooded compartment."

"I don't really believe in the possibility of opening the escape hatch, but if they say so, they should be helped," I say to the Old Man.

The captain waited impatiently for the opportunity to get acquainted with the situation on the ship. He was under pressure from Commander Nills Ganas, the Canadian Navy rescue coordinator, who finally officially declared the sunken submarine to be HMCS Corner Draak (SSK-264) of the Royal Canadian Navy. However, it will be about 16 hours before the rescue ship is next to us. Much faster, in just four hours, the Sub Marine Parachute Assistance Group (SPAG) announced its arrival, with a standby time of four to six hours. It is a special rescue group specializing in helping sunken submarines around the world. After landing on the surface of the water at the accident site, parachute groups will help those who have decided to leave the submarine on their own. However, I hope that will not happen, because this operation it's too dangerous. Commander Pardy Ryan Commander and Coordinator in the rescue operation of the SPAG group, emphasizes the need to take into account psychological aspects. Liaison with the crew inside the sunken ship keeps them hopeful. They announced on the radio that they had SEIE suits, which made it possible for the crew to leave the damaged ship safely. They also considered the possibility of dropping the suits from the plane, but we do not have divers to oversee the evacuation of the crew. It would take a minimum of three and I was alone. Jarek had to supervise the hose with forced air, so the idea was abandoned. With this accent the captain ended his brief speech to the crew.

I went down to the water with the end of the cable attached to a special buoy. While I was in the decompression chamber, our tug made a few maneuvers and positioned itself over the sunken ship. So I didn't have to use now with the help of a pontoon to go down - straight to its hull. Guided by Jarek's air supply hoses, I quickly found myself beside him. I caught a glimpse of his satisfied gaze as I tapped my hand on his helmet glass. Two people are always brighter under water. Holding the end of the cable in my hand, I showed him that I wanted to plug it into the socket.

Jarek, slowly walking in his lead shoes, walked in front of me towards the conning tower.

"They must hear his lead shoes click," I thought.

There, next to the combat conning tower connecting to the hull, about two meters from the escape hatch, I saw the characteristic marking of the compressed air link.

Jarek reached down and lifted the cover, revealing the hermetic socket connector. I plugged my tip into it and locked the cover firmly. Now only the link is sucked out by "Poseidon" and the air can be forced inside the hull. Of course, if there is no mechanical damage somewhere along the way. I swam to the emergency hatch, wondering if it was possible to get in. There was such a possibility, but I needed outside help.

I showed Jarek with my hand that I was going to go inside the ship.

Having voice communication with Poseidon, I coordinate our attempts to open the escape hatch. I'm fucking scared of being stuck there forever. My only comfort is the fact that my sixth sense hasn't spoken from the very beginning. It's a good sign. Jarek turned his huge steel head towards me and, with a smile on his lips, pointed his thumb down. Then he patted my shoulder as if to comfort me, knowing my fears. I hear clicks from inside the ship, I know Jarek cannot hear them, but he already knows that the escape hatch is flooded because I can see him saying to me: "Get in."

He opens the large escape hatch without difficulty and looks inside, waving his hand at me. I hovered over her and he, with a sly smile on his lips, placed his hand on my head and pushed me in. After a while, I felt the resistance of the bottom of the hatch under my feet. Before I could realize it, flap over my head snapped shut.

Darkness enveloped me. I turned on my flashlight. At face level, I see some valve connectors, next to it a few tube inlets and outlets, some two and a half inches long.

Air started blowing rapidly from one of them, I felt the pressure change and the water around me began to diminish. After a long while the hatch was dry. I stood at the edge of the hatch, looking down. I thought there was a second hatch, but I was wrong. It wasn't there, but I heard a metallic click, and a semicircular gate opened on my right side. I saw two sailors standing next to it. They quickly grabbed my arms and helped me out from the hatch.

In the light of the lit flashlights, I can see the submarines gathered in the command post. Their smiling faces express hope of survival. My presence here is a very important psychological aspect. They know that if someone from outside came to them on a damaged ship, that is, the possibility of leaving it safely.

The commander, Commander Harry Montery, is talking to our captain right now. When he sees me, he says hello and gives me the telephone receiver, simultaneously switching his voice to the emergency intercom. Now the whole crew can hear what are we talking about.

"Ryszard, when you are there, try to get to the room with the oxygen cylinders they have." The captain confirmed the news that they have over a dozen sets of breathing apparatus. We can get some people out of the ship.

"Can the wounded reach the surface in oxygen devices without thermal suits?" he asks.

"If they are conscious and able to stand alone in the hatch, then yes."

A commander from the Command of the Canadian Rescue Team intervenes in the conversation in Polish:

"Speak English," he asks.

The captain reports further doubts in English.

"We pump the air to the maximum, it should be enough until a specialized rescue ship arrives."

"Do you feel a blast of clean air there?" he asks.

"No, I don't feel like that yet, but I'm too short here to say it. However, they have control apparatuses here, and oxygen saturation seems to be steadily, albeit slowly, improving."

I report to the Old Man that, according to my pressure gauge, the ship has a pressure of 4.5 bar.

"I have forty-three minutes. Then I have to go back because I'm going to occupy the decompression chamber. And they will need the chamber more."

"Okay, act and report the effects. We discuss with the captain of the ship how to get there to compartment four and check on the rest of the crew."

"Theoretically it's possible. There would practically have to be at least three of us here. However, you need to know the layout of the rooms for the OP. Without it, it is dangerous and impossible by one person," I talk to him. "Do you have any trained scuba divers?" I ask.

"No, it so happens that they may be in the fourth compartment. If they did," he added quietly.

"That's bad," I don't know the ship. I don't know how to get around. Plus the darkness and the lack of time.

"I understand, but it's a simple road. You can do it!" He convinces me.

"Did they give any signals that they were alive? Maybe they tapped?"

"Yes, at first there was a clicking noise."

"Now silence? Until the moment when you communicated with us? Captain, there are people in the fourth compartment, maybe Jarek will go to the fourth compartment and try to contact them somehow. Air has to be delivered there."

Reporting to the captain about the new arrangements, I handed the phone back to the commander of the ship, and myself, with the help of one sailor, I went to the sunken compartment, where the nearest storage with breathing apparatus is located. Every exit from the Ship's Commanding Center a poses an additional risk of poisonous vapors from flooded batteries and smoke getting inside from a fire in burnt rooms. First we enter the vestibule of the corridor, here we have to put on masks and breathe air from cylinders or emergency devices. Behind us are large, round steel doors of the watertight bulkhead. The center is a separate room on the ship - something like a completely independent large kingston recessed into the hull of a submarine. Its only job is to isolate this room away from the rest of the ship in the event of fire or flooding. It is the "last resort" where the crew gathers and waits for outside help. The situation is still serious, but no longer dire. Now that the danger of a shortage of air has been averted and it is forced in, the question of increased pressure remains, for more than half of the ship is flooded with water. Sea water flooded the battery banks, from where the deadly chlorine is slowly but steadily spreading. Oxygen, Carbon Dioxide, and Carbon Monoxide, and Chlorine - these are the four most common resulting gases as a result of a fire, they are under constant control in the Center.

All indicators controlling their level are stuck in the yellow alarm field. However, none of them reached the red - critical - level that would force the crew to evacuate immediately. We open the hatch leading to the corridor, where at the end, but one level below, there is a storage with twenty-eight cylinders of oxygen. They are emergency breathing apparatus designed to protect the person using them for two hours of breathing. They also allow him to enter the escape hatch and surfacing. Not from every depth, of course, but the thirty-odd meters they're stuck at is within their reach. I slowly follow the sailor, and the way is illuminated by the dim light from the ship's flashlights.

We stand above the descent, the hatch securing the hatch is open, and the oily surface of the water flashes beneath it in the beam of lights. He can't go in there - his breathing apparatus is not designed to work underwater.

I go down alone. Ten meters straight down the corridor, then another ten on the left and there is a storage that interests us - I repeat his directions in my mind. I do not put on fins - I will not swim, but walk on the deck. I find the storage without any problems and take two apparatuses from the shelves. I can't do more. One is slung over my shoulder and the other is dragged all the way back. I must go back now. I'm running out of air and the maximum time I can be at this depth. With two apparatus, they'll get the rest themselves from the storage when the need arises. However, I do not know if it will be necessary and safe - the water is only four degrees. High command agreed that eleven people could evacuate through the escape hatch to our decompression chamber. The rest of the apparatuses are to constitute a safety reserve for the remaining members of the ship. We quickly agreed that I would secure the first two submarines and swim to the surface with him. These are the most stressed and slightly injured sailors with arm and leg fractures and general bruises.

Captain P., having seen the list of crew in the command compartment, suggests going out as the first ship's doctor.

"We do not have a doctor on board," he argues, "and he will certainly be needed during the evacuation of the wounded, they need professional help," he adds.

The doctor was ordered to leave second - right behind me.

I was the first to go inside the hatch and the first to leave, checking the operation of the escape hatch - this is my task - I think about those cold seamen sitting in the dark. I go inside the escape hatch - its chamber is dry. Now they close the hatch beneath me, and after a while I see it filling up quickly with water. When the water pressure equalized with the pressure outside, the emergency hatch opens and I see the silhouette of Jarek standing and insures my exit. Bingo! I look at my watch - it took me several dozen seconds. Now the next one. We're waiting at the conning tower next to the trapdoor. The hatch slowly opens and we pull the doctor outside. He's frightened, he's cold, and his teeth are clutching the air mouthpiece so hard that I'm afraid he'll bite it off. The mask is flooded with water; he can't get rid of it and it stresses him a lot. I hold him tight. It calms him down a little. I tie it with my rope and we splash upwards together. There they immediately grab his hands and quickly enter the chamber.

How long did it take? I look at the stopwatch of my watch. In 20 seconds - 38 meters, good time. I go back to Jarek. The second appears. I think he has a broken left leg, because, somehow unnaturally twisted to the side, it prevents him from leaving the hatch. I also tie this to myself and up quickly. 28 seconds - a little more. I changed the cylinder set and went down to Jarek's again. The wounded man took the heat shock badly, he was all blue and in convulsions, he quickly found himself in the chamber, where the doctor treated him. Not good - it could end badly for someone. The captain noticed it too - he was standing by the side and looked at him. He ordered the suspension of further evacuation. This emergency exit is a last resort and should be avoided. The water's too cold and they're stressed out. But we understood their urge to evacuate.

Once he is on the surface, he will be safe. But that wasn't the whole truth. There were many dangers for them here.

One of the highlights now was cold water and thermal shock. If you can leave with decompression stops, this is the only way back. But that's not all - and there are a number of factors here. They can't decompress as much time as they should. They have been under increased pressure for too long, so I understood well our captain's decision. We heard the news that the fourth compartment does not have a connection for pumping compressed air from the outside. You have to come up with something else. Providing Jarek with the raised thumb of my right hand, the information that everything is OK with me, I moved fighting downstream to the starboard side of the ship. I wanted to check something. A few years back as part of the Polish MW exercises and the Polish Ship Rescue with the Danish Navy, I emerged from their submarine to the surface through a torpedo tube. It wasn't particularly complicated, but it did require the coordination of the crew.

Perhaps it is possible now, but the other way around, I thought as I headed for his four starboard torpedo tubes. Three of them were closed, but the fourth had the hatch open. It was empty. Something loomed to me then under the hull of the ship, I swam closer to the bottom to the very hatch of the launcher and I looked down. Chain! The old, rusty chain is pressed to the bottom by the ship's hull!

How did it come from here? I didn't have time to think when my sixth sense kicked in.

Not good, but what and where?

In order not to fight the current, I grabbed the trapdoor with one hand. I followed the chain with my eyes. There's something there, but what? Too far for me to say what it is. I pulled a safety line through some eye in the hull and locked the latch. Now, releasing it, I moved away from the hull, following the chain lower and lower. Here the bottom descended more steeply into the depths of the ocean. I can't go deeper, I thought. But I can see that it is not far away so I moved a few more meters and with horror I saw a brown and black lump with some tentacles growing out of its spherical body. I wipe the mask with my hand - I wanted to wipe the sweat that poured on my forehead. It's such an unconditional reflex at the sight of that enormous expression. I got goosebumps all over my body. I can already guess what caused the disaster of this submarine. Such mines from World War II were dropped into the water in pairs. Chained together, they swam somewhere at different depths, waiting patiently for a ship or warship to attach to the chain and pull them to its hull.

And then, hitting the hull with their insets, they exploded from both sides, giving no chance to such a poor man. This one was floating about three meters above the bottom, torn by the current that was pulling her. I swim closer to the point where the bottom blows steeply down a rock slope as wide as my field of view. How much can it be? Fifty, seventy meters? Or more, but I can't judge it.

I swim even closer, passing a mine in the distance several meters, now it is below me and behind my back. I now stick to the same depth all the time, on what the submarine lies. I was about to turn my back on cliffs and come back as I watched in a fit of intuition down straight under you. No, it's impossible, I think I have some hallucinations...

"What the hell is this?" I wonder.

The bottom under me was littered with slightly swaying round pots that look like poppyhead, which have lost their flowers and are standing in the field waiting for someone will tear them off. All lean towards the pusher eats the current, but resisting its strength and still stuck in it same place. Some lower, very close to the bottom, and others a little higher. Throughout the middle of this "poppy field" there is a carved road that looks as if it is large the reaper went from the ocean side to the very escarpment and stripped the field of poppies twenty, maybe a little more meters. It all looked like a dam guarding who knows what. Their regular arrangement told me that it was not nature, but human hand makes this shape. But what is it and what is it here for? - I wonder.

Holding the lifeline tightly, I float down the slope upside down to the bottom. I am so close to the rocks that I can touch them with my hand. The underwater river must hit this rock chasm, and it rushes on, increasing its speed as it throws me like a flag in the wind.

"Just for this rock breach," I say to myself. "It's not far, maybe ten meters. I will see what is there next," I cannot easily cover this distance.

I look down; the bottom from the side of the escarpment falls steeply towards the ocean, and in a rocky precipice, about a hundred meters from me, I notice a black, several dozen meters large gap in this solid rock. All this in the faint glow of the day breaking through here. Slightly vibrating rays of the sun break in this current and blur this image for me. The road through the "poppy field" leads to this rock chasm.

I was about to descend even lower, curious about what I saw when my sixth sense spoke again:

"Stop," I heard an inner voice.

In the distance, by the rift in the rock, a green airy form of the Almond Apparition appeared to me.

I immediately stuck to the rocky cliff. I felt a slight tug - it was over lifeline. I have to go back, I thought, looking at the underwater river that passed me by. Was she the one who carved that hole in the rock? - I wonder.

I could detach from the line and swim a little lower, but I'm without Jarek, so I'd better come back, maybe it's time to take a closer look at it later. I also never disregarded my inner voice - my sixth sense, as I called it. Why is there only one mine here? - I think, watching the one below me pulsate with electricity. Working hard with my fins and helping myself to pull the safety line, I slowly but steadily approach the ship. Once I got to its hull, I was pretty tired from this way back. Near me, on the upper deck above the torpedo tubes,

Jarek was standing and playing the director, filming the entire hull of the ship with our "burrower".

I swam up to him. "Follow me!" I wave to him. I know he has connection to Poseidon and that I will be visible there. Jarek was not as mobile and efficient as I was. His deep-sea outfit restricted his movements and slowed his steps. He wasn't swimming - he was walking. The camera, pushed by the strong current, was slipping from his hands as he tried to show the open torpedo tube. He grabbed one of the cables and pulled it off back to himself. The camera cables in a semicircular arc pushed by the water current shot upwards, towards the surface, mixing with the bubbles of air escaping from our suits. I take the camera and direct her eye to the mine. I don't know how it will be visible there, but it will surely attract their attention. As it turned out later, on "Poseidon" they did not know what it was, but having received through the Internet everything that our camera was filming, Canadians easily - enlarging and processing the shot of this mass by computer - they recognized that it was a mine from the Second World War. They transmit this information via intercom to Jarek, so he nods to me and points upstairs. I come to the surface. Jarek is right behind me. We have to think about what to do next. The explosion of such a mine will kill all divers within a radius of many hundreds of meters from it. What will happen to the ship is difficult to predict, but nothing good for sure. And Canadian rescuers will land here soon.

"They'd better be safe," says the captain. In our little dive room brainstorm continues. The case was settled by Jarek:

"I'll go down and burn the chain," I declare.

"Let them hold the other end of this chain from the pontoon, so that it does not run away and hit the rock chasm."

"Yes, this is a good solution, and a special buoy with satellite signaling and a few floats can be attached to the mine, let it flow afterwards."

The captain passed this suggestion to the Canadians.

"If you have the opportunity, act. A buoy with position signaling will allow you to locate it and destroy it from the air right after you release it and it will be in a safe distance for you," said the Commander of the Battle Ships Flotilla, Commander Peter Wilson.

"Okay, don't talk anymore. I go down - you hear Jarek's voice. "It's late and we still have a lot to do."

Jarek goes underwater again - how long is it submerged? I get nervous so I check in a dive log kept by the third officer very meticulously. Maybe a little more, I can too, I say, reassured.

We pass the cables with the burner to the boatswain on our motorboat. Just a positional signal buoy from our left wing and Jarek goes to action. Our camera landed on the submarine and rigidly attached by Jarek to his snore, it showed us a face. First, Jarek descended as carefully as his stiff suit would allow him and hooked the end of a strong nylon cord to the rusty chain. The other end of the line was crowned on the surface our rescue buoy and the five big orange floats the boatswain had picked up from the storage. Then, walking along the bottom at the chain, returned to the ship's hull. There he took the burner and in a couple of minutes cut the chain. Mine jumped a few meters up and went downstream towards the open ocean, disappearing to us out of sight. We saw it dragging a buoy that started broadcasting her position on the rescue channel, and five orange floats kept her on constant depth.

"The helicopter has already taken off," the captain told us, who, in contact with the Rescue Center, received this information from Canadians.

"I'm going into the water. I will go inside the ship, maybe I can get to the fourth compartment," I say to the captain after studying the layout of the rooms on the ship. I noticed that the fourth torpedo compartment is on the same level as the third torpedo tube. I got dressed and went to Jarek's. I had something else to do there. I swim over to him and showed him my watch, then five fingers.

Understood - five minutes - I read his lips. I nod my head in agreement. I take a small metal hammer from his belt bag.

He had no idea what I was going to do, so he looked at me puzzled, wondering what the hammer was for. Because it's impossible to swim inside the torpedo tube with two bottles on my back, I take them off and hold them in front of me. I can see the camera eye following my movements.

The Old Man's gonna be pissed off now, I think. But he will not take me back, there is no communication with me.

He knows perfectly well what I am going to do, he took part in these sea maneuvers with me, literally - he did not dive with me, but he was the Chief on Neptune at the time, who secured the whole exercises and safeguarded our actions.

Slowly, holding the bottles in front of me and the mouthpiece with air in my teeth, I slide them into the dark opening of the torpedo tube. Then, fighting the flow, I swim after them. Silence and darkness enveloped me. I reach for my left forearm and unhook the flashlight from the Velcro. A strong beam of light diffuses the darkness prevailing here. How many meters can a torpedo have? - I try to remember. Three or a little more? Two flaps of his fins and I hear a click. It was the cylinder that hit into the inner hatch. I crouch my legs and brace my elbows against the round, smooth sides of the launch pad. I tap the hammer on the wall of the launcher, the signal known to every sailor - S.O.S., I repeat it again and again.

Is there a sunken compartment behind it or not?

There are sailors there who heard the knocking, I think, waiting for the distinctive sound of the front launcher hatch closing.

Silence. A long silence. I was about to roll back outside when I felt a slight current of water - it was the closing hatch that added a little pressure to the launch tube. They close it - I managed to think, when I heard the characteristic hiss of the air pushing the water out of the chamber, they began to slowly drain it, equalizing the pressure to that of the ship. A soft crack and the hatch in front of me has been opened, and some hands are pulling me inside, pulling the bottles, which I hold with outstretched hands. It couldn't be otherwise - no water, no swimming or crawling - it's too tight for that. They gently bring me upright. Two submarines wearing masks on their heads with square air purifying kits on their backs grab tanks and want to put them on my back. But I have to get rid of the fins first - you can't walk in them. I take them off and put them on my shoulder. I grab the cylinders and bend under their weight, they weigh nothing in the water, but here a lot. Seeing this, one of the sailors comes up to me and helps me bear them. They lead me to the slightly opened hatch, from which we are illuminated by the light of flashlights. When we finally get out of this compartment, they slam the hatch and lock it tight. They don't take their masks off yet, so neither do I. However, I noticed in fact, I felt in my ears that the pressure inside the ship was not less than that in the water when I entered the launcher.

"Not good, damn, very bad. This complicates the rescue tremendously," I thought, looking at my blood pressure monitor: 5.1 bar. This is a bad signal for me. I am also concerned with the laws of physics. There can be many hazards on a damaged submarine, one of which is pressure.

Ideally, it should not be larger than on the surface. But there it is - these 5.1 bar are about forty-one meters deep.

If the submarine is partially flooded, and its crew stays under such pressure for a long time, it takes a minimum of 40 hours for decompression. Flooding the compartment in which the crew is located with water cause the pressure in it increases, and the seamen inside become "divers" as they do now. The pressure, depth, and time spent in this place pose a risk of decompression sickness. Last but not least, the increased pressure causes an increase in the partial pressure of other gases in the atmosphere of this room, which will certainly create an additional threat to life. In the event of a battery flooding with seawater, oxygen, carbon dioxide and carbon monoxide, when they are not constantly monitored - and it may be that there is no such possibility - become a sudden and inevitable cause of death.

In such a situation, immediate evacuation is the solution.

Is it possible? We all wondered recently.

One and perhaps the most important reason for preventing immediate evacuation is the water temperature, which is only four degrees Celsius. If they have thermal suits like me, or if I can provide them, they have a chance of surviving at that temperature. That's what I'm here for - to create this opportunity. Only for two and a half hour - this is the time left before the parachute rescue unit arrives - specialist life suits will be at their disposal. Do they have enough time to wait? They didn't! This I understood immediately when I looked at the control apparatus. They knew it too.

This is the first threat. The second is the number of people that our decompression chamber can accommodate - certainly not all, or even a negligible part of them, considering even the option of stuffing them like herring in a can.

I would not like to be in the shoes of our captain. He is now in charge of the rescue operation and makes decisions.

What will it take now? - I wonder. The sailors follow me to the room, in which most of the crew were gathered. It is cold, very cold - I can see it from their cold hands lit by short flashes of flashlights. Thirty-eight people - so many of them saved. I quickly calculate: each five to eight minutes for a possible evacuation. It's five hours. God - and they are already in the purification apparatuses. We won't make it, there's no chance they'll have enough air left. I am dragged to the only portable CO2 device in air. It's hanging on a pipe. Damn! The pointer catches on the red area. They all sit on the deck. They have enough room for themselves here, but because there are so many of them and they are under more pressure, the oxygen depletes faster than that in the command compartment.

How to give them oxygen? - I think intensely.

One of the mechanics wrapped in a silver fire blanket waves his hands in front of my eyes, finally grabs my elbow and pulls me towards the flooded corridor. They don't say anything to me. They cannot take off their masks or they could pass out immediately. I take a long breath of air and hand the mouthpiece to the mechanic. He takes three deep breaths and says to me in a raised voice:

"There is oxygen!" points down at the flooded hatch in the corridor, "you need to unscrew the valves."

He puts on his mask again. Meanwhile, I inhale the air from the cylinder and give him the mouthpiece again.

"Eight enormous cylinders of ballast air in a flooded part of the engine room, forty or so meters away," he says quickly.

He can't do more and he gives me the mouthpiece. We repeat the entire operation three more times.

Ryszard was afraid. He didn't know which side the danger was on. His sixth sense gave him no sign of threatening him, only he was in danger. Now he had to figure out how much to risk for himself. He has air in his cylinders for about an hour, they only have half. Going down was not too difficult. However, it is unassisted by a second diver, and this is always dangerous. But he realized that if he didn't do something, they might all be dead in twenty minutes and no one will have to let him go. Involuntarily, he was in the same position as them. He decided to come in.

He took out his mouthpiece and called out:

"The plan! Draw me a plan to get those cylinders there!"

The mechanic was quickly given a notebook and on a piece of paper he drew a descent down, and then a wide room, from which there are two corridors to the left and right: left and right. About eleven yards from the fork, there are four bottles by each wall. Eight large air cylinders in total. But that's not the end of the problem.

The mechanic draws where there are two snakes that need to be connected to a certain place.

"Here," the valve on the pipe is marked with a cross. "Opposite each other are two valves. Attach the hose to one of them and pull the end out to them. You can do it?"

He writes next to it on a piece of paper.

"I'll try," I write back.

Ryszard looks at the drawing for a moment longer. He has to remember everything right away, there will be no time for any revisions. Patted on the shoulder by the second mechanic, he goes down into the water down the engine room, with his soul on his shoulder, thinking only of the Almond Apparition that loomed in the distance. He raises his hand when he sees her and mentally asks her for help. He had never done this, but now he was afraid. Why is Jarek not with me? He wondered. He descended slowly, the darkness engulfing him lit up with a flashlight in his right hand. He looked in all directions as he swam along the lower deck. "I can't hook anything," he said to himself in his mind. His large flashlight illuminated the space in front of him, leaving black masses of water agitated by his fins behind him. His left hand was constantly groping the floor of the room, telling his senses what horizontal position he was in. Water mixed with some rusty bloom did not encourage further penetration of the interior. There were torn pipes, sheets of metal and other things everywhere. He came to a fork. It was safer here - the shock wave spread to the sides, losing its destructive power.

That's when he saw him - damn it! He didn't write this to me. After a while, one more and a few more. They were all horribly burned above the deck, stuck at the very top of the room, in which it was located. Dark thoughts about the danger lurking in some nook and cranny overwhelmed his consciousness. The cold shook his whole body, then he felt hot sweat flooding him.

Instinctively, he glanced at the phosphorescent air gauge.

"He's half way through. Good," he thought, relaxing.

He looked around - these cylinders must already be here somewhere. Some devices passed by - not telling him too much pumps or something. No, it must be centrifuges. He was distracting his thoughts from the bodies of drowned people before him.

"They are here!" He rejoiced when he saw in the beam of his flashlight four huge cylinders of air. He thought for a moment, recalling the image in his mind from the card. Now hoses, he started thinking about hoses. Where the hell are they? They were supposed to hang on some pipes six meters to the right. But there's nothing there!

What to do? He wondered nervously, shining his flashlight around. It was not that simple - there was no top and bottom here, only darkness. The darkness around made it impossible to locate. He had to illuminate the space every now and then to check where he was.

"I will look for a while, and if I don't find them, I will go back to the other corridor, maybe they will be there," he was saying to himself.

Then he saw them. They were lying nearby, on some engine, thrown there by the force of an explosion. The burnt rubber on the hoses was visible here and there with a metal protective mesh.

He quickly threw them over his shoulder and, so weighed down, had to slowly walk along the deck with short jumps towards the collecting connector for these cylinders. The water in which he moved was not clean - it was contaminated with oils, fuel, various garbage was floating in it and items. He was moving in a strange position. The snakes, quite heavy, were pulling him down. Catching on anything stable, he pulled himself forward, leaning sharply towards the deck. And so on again and again. It was easy for him to connect the end of the hose to the valve. The snap link snapped instantly.

He grabbed the other free end and pulled it toward the fork.

Here he had to face these unfortunates again.

"There is no way to help them anymore," he thought, but for those upstairs there is definitely an opportunity.

Sailing faster along the already cleared road, he swam out into a companionway with the end of the hose in his hand. "Here you go!" He waved his hand to the mechanic who was bent over the descent to the engine room. He came back the same way and turned on the taps of all four cylinders. The hose stiffened and rose up. Salvation air began to spread throughout the room. He repeated the whole operation again in the second corridor. Now, however, he had to grab with his own hands the drowned sailor blocking his way. He got stuck between the fallen pipes. It illuminated his face. It was calm, he looked like he had fallen asleep. He felt very sad.

"The young boy tragically ended his service to his homeland. Will the motherland make it up to his family?"

He thought as he grabbed his trouser belt and gently pulled him away from the narrow passage.

Having swam to the companionway, he himself left with the other end of the hose in his hand. Removing his fins, he headed for the gauge. The pointer definitely fell to half the yellow field. He thought again about the Almond Apparition. "Something was wrong with it all. The air for the ballasts filled their room. That's good - it's definitely not harmful. But what about carbon dioxide?" He wondered. He didn't run anywhere, he had nowhere, he is still here. "Doesn't that pose some risk of poisoning when the crew takes off their CO2 absorber masks?"

While thinking about it, he kept the mouthpiece from his mouth, just in case. He looked at the air gauge of his cylinders again. The pointer was relentlessly approaching the reserve.

"We must go out, I did my best," he thought.

Illuminated and admired by submarines, he tried to show them that he had to return to the surface. His heart rejoiced as he saw the hope seep into them back. They don't have to die anymore - they can now wait for rescue.

On a piece of paper he quickly wrote to them:

"Help on the way. Canadian rescue teams will be here in an hour. Wait! I have to go to the surface. Fast!!!!!" He put a few exclamation points.

The same sailors followed him to the smoky room, to the third torpedo tube. First the bottles, then he squeezed into her narrow, round opening, praying that everything would go well.

With a hammer he tapped out a rhythm known to Jarek - a Polish children's rhyme. He didn't know why he did it. Jarek couldn't hear it anyway.

It went well and in a moment he was landing in his embrace. After a while, Jarek released him and showed him his watch with rapid movements of his hand.

Helplessly spreading his hands, Ryszard replied with a gesture that there was nothing he could do about it.

The colleagues at the top rose to the occasion. Two air cylinders dangled from the first decompression bench.

He sat down on it and all the tension was gone. He wanted to cry and it was only the fact that he was wearing a mask on his face that made him not to cry. Why was he so reacting to his exploits? He didn't know, and he didn't care. He was alone. Jarek also had to come back to the surface. Both of them had long exceeded all time limits for a safe stay underwater. Today it was their last descent into the water. Or so they thought now.

Ryszard comes out a bit slower than Jarek, who, with the camera in his hand, passes him on the last decompression bench. Once it's three meters below the surface, another half an hour waits. Staring from below into the sun-shimmering turquoise surface of the water, he notices shadows moving rapidly across it. These are the silhouettes of parachute-landing divers. Immediately behind them, three huge dinghies fall to the surface with a loud splash. The crew from the first response parachute rescue team landed in the water, dropped from the plane with all its equipment.

The dark shadows of their pontoons swinging in the wave can be seen near the hull. Now they are taking over further rescue operations. Staring at the surface of the water, he receives a sign that it is now safe to return to the tug. He comes out slowly and climbs on board,

Where he quickly dumps all his gear. He sees irritated that the "searchlight" has focused its eye on him. He quickly disappears from his sight, approaching his colleagues waiting next to him. Almost the entire crew is waiting there, and Cook approaches him with a cup of strong black coffee.

"Where's the chocolate?" Ryszard asks more out of defiance than out of real need.

"It is here, it is, you deserve it. I'll get it right now," and he's off to his kingdom.

He must have looked weird because they were watching him anxiously.

The Bo'sun first sensed that there was something wrong with him. He patted him gently on the back, saying in a concerned voice:

"It's okay, it'll be okay."

Ryszard did not speak at all. He didn't say what he had been doing for so long. The captain also sensed his gloomy mood, because he said to him:

"Just tell me if they're alive."

"They're alive. Thirty-eight people. They are alive and they will live to be saved, but the others will not," he replied.

"Go, rest a bit, then come and report back. If we need you, we'll call you."

He went to the cabin. He didn't feel like talking to anyone.

# Chapter VI

# Assist

The commander of their group landed in the water with the paratroopers. The office in Gdynia agreed to the further assistance of "Poseidon" in the rescue operation, so Captain P. invited the commander to our tugboat, from where he will be able to command the rescue operation until the Canadian specialist unit arrives.

"They'll be there in a few hours," he told us as he came aboard.

He made himself at home in the dive room, where he appreciated that our camera would provide an invaluable service in coordinating activities.

"Glad to hear it, but what does the commander expect of us?" The captain asked.

"Take the most harmed on a tug and place them in a decompression chamber."

"We have six SEIE suits and we'll evacuate them to your deck, one by one."

"Will you also provide us with a heavy diving suit and provide its service?" The commander asked.

"Each of my people is a trained diver," added. "So it will be faster. They also cannot be constantly in the water, and with the diver, the evacuation will be faster."

"Of course, please have everything what we have," our Old Man assured him.

The commander notified the crew of the submarine, that is in place with first flush of lifeguards and proceed to evacuate the most injured. He asked the captain of the ship to select the first six crew members for evacuation. We all heard thunderous applause and voices of joy coming from within the ship.

"How did you find our ship?" That was the first question the commander asked us, looking at the monitor screen. "We've been looking for it for several hours and despite all the technology at our disposal, we haven't found it."

"We didn't find it," our captain replied.

"How is it: not you?" The commander was surprised.

"It was the whales that found it and brought us to it."

The commander looked at the Old Man with astonished eyes, not understanding anything.

When the captain told him how we got here, he shook his head in disbelief.

"It's a strange story! Nobody would believe it if it weren't true. How little we still know about the inhabitants of these waters..." he added thoughtfully.

The camera, meanwhile, showed us as two divers with two SEIE suits prepared to enter through the emergency hatch. This rescue suit is currently used in over twenty fleets around the world and could once again save the crew from a sunken submarine. The evacuation itself is not too complicated. A designated sailor puts on the SEIE suit and fastens the zipper as in a regular jacket. To the emergency hatch exit is entered individually. After entering, the side or bottom hatch cover is closed behind it. One of his tasks, which no one can do for him, is to connect to the connector supplying the suit with air. The suit fills up quickly and the excess air escapes through special valves. An evacuee hears a leak of compressed air. The next step is to fill the escape hatch with seawater. Pressure in the evacuation shaft remains unchanged (excess air escapes through the valve in the suit shaft) until the water reaches the evacuated chest level. At this point, the relief valve closes and water continues to flow into the well, doubling the pressure every four seconds. The evacuee must still be connected with the supply system, breathe regularly, maintaining the proper tidal volume in the lungs, and equalize the pressure in the eustachian tubes by performing swallowing reflexes. This is when the pressure outside the ship is different than inside it. Faster pressurization and shorter pressurization times mean a lower risk of DCS as less nitrogen enters the blood and tissues. After the pressure is equalized with the outboard ship, the upper hatch cover opens. The suit immediately rises to the surface. The suit's large displacement allows for its quick departure.

Here, from a depth of 34 meters, it took approx. 9 seconds. The evacuator was immediately sent to the decompression chamber, and his suit to the next rescuing sailor.

In this case, the pressure in the submarine was less than half a bar less than at a depth of 40 meters on which their submarine lay. Fourteen hours in such conditions gave no chance for any of them to survive without decompression in the chamber. Then the hatch was prepared for the next evacuation. Within five minutes, the hatch to the ship's hatch was drained and depressurized, and another crewman entered the hatch.

When I entered the dive room, our captain introduced me briefly to the commander:

"This is Richard."

The commander got up, saluted me then shook my hand, saying:

"Thank you on behalf of myself and on behalf of the entire Canadian Navy."

I shrugged my shoulders and replied:

"Anyone would do it in my place."

"Not true, not many would decide to do that," he answered me in a serious voice, adding immediately: "I know what I am saying, I have been working in this profession for many years."

Flooded with such praise, spoken in front of the entire crew, I proudly looked around, but immediately added:

"It's thanks to our captain. If it weren't for him, I wouldn't be there."

The rescue operation was gaining momentum. We were just observers now. Jarek assisted in putting on our equipment one of the parachute group, and I stood leaning on the railing and watching the efficient action of their divers. In fact, they could do without us. Their pontoons were equipped with everything that was needed for the efficient and safe evacuation of sailors from a sunken submarine - except for a decompression chamber. But this one was already approaching with the Canadian rescue ship.

The conversations coming from the loudspeaker showed that in the bow compartment and in the command compartment amidships there are rescuers who direct the evacuation of sailors, taking care of their safety and order during evacuation.

The first of the crew have already landed in our chamber. There are already four of them there. Time spent in the coordination center is being calculated. Using the data provided by the rescuers, we calculate that they must stay there for about a dozen or so hours. That's a lot. The only consolation is that in eight hours on the Canadian rescue vessel there will be enough space for all 54 seafarers who still have to wait patiently. It would seem that everything is on track, but it was not.

"The ship is changing position," we heard one voice of lifeguards.

A moment of consternation and wondering what is causing it.

"Why did it move? It's flooded!" The commander wonders.

"I know why," I said aloud, turning my head towards our captain.

"Speak," he said.

"I opened eight large cylinders of ballast air, and their contents filled the entire bow compartment and beyond, the air must have burst into other parts of the ship and changed its displacement," I explain my actions to them. "Now it is more susceptible to the effects of water current."

During this time, no one was interested in why the sailors in the forward compartment did not suffocate due to lack of air. And in the rush of the Canadian rescue team, no one asked me what I was doing there. Only now did I get the alert from the Almond Apparition. That's it - the ship is about to move into the depths of several hundred meters.

The captain of "Poseidon", having imagined the situation, makes the only possible decision:

"Commander, is it possible to attach our tow to the ship?" he asks.

A quick look at the submarine situational plan on the table.

"It is possible, it has a towing eye on the bow," replies the commander.

"What are you going to do?"

"We'll take it in tow and hold it. I won't get it to the surface, but maybe I'll prevent it from sliding down the underwater slope."

The Old Man takes the microphone and orders:

"Crew to positions. Bo'sun: prepare the tow to be served."

"Water diver," he says to the commander. "Fast. Everyone hurried away to their activities. Towing a sunken submarine."

We haven't done that yet - I think. But it may be the only way.

"Two lifeguards to the side, a water diver, now!" this time the commander seems to give instructions to his people. "Do not stop the evacuation, speed up the extraction of people as much as possible," he orders. Meanwhile, we advise the captain on how to secure "Poseidon" during this operation.

We must be able to cut off the tow immediately in case we fail and the ship starts to drag us into the water. This version should also be considered.

"Captain, if he starts to drag us, we won't be able to start the tow." There will be no time for this," says the boatswain.

"What do you suggest?"

"We've got a bit of a broken tow here, about three hundred meters. Let the divers attach its end to the ship, and we will polish it on board in such a way that it can be disposed of in a few seconds.

"Third!" the Captain calls to our "barker".

"How's the calculations?"

On the bridge, the Third fights with logarithms and, hitting the computer keyboard, tries to calculate what forces will be acting on us as the ship glides into the depths.

"Captain - this is reading cards. Not enough data. I do not know the amount of water the ship has taken in, or its displacement. From the fact that he started, it should be concluded that it is almost zero, but there is also this current and a steep bottom."

"Stop talking, just say, can we make it?" Keep interrupts him.

"If we have to drag him up the bottom, we will not be able to," he replies cautiously.

"And if we are supposed to just hold it?"

"It should be fine as long as the weather doesn't change," said Third, and a sigh of relief escaped from his chest.

"Commander, here we go," the captain said, stepping up close and looking at the monitor.

"Richard, you will come down again, but not for a long time," says the Old Man. "You must be there when lifeguards engage the lobby. Just for this time. If we are to succeed, it must be properly attached," he adds.

"I'm going," I muttered to him, and waved my hand to Jarek. "Come on, help me get dressed."

I can see how, not far from us, three pontoons joined together and created a base for evacuees from a ship of sailors. Hence, one of the pontoons quickly delivered them to our chamber.

"Nine seconds to leave plus ten to enter the chamber. It's OK, they'll be fine," I say loudly to Jarek. After three minutes I was in the water.

Shit, for such crap money such a job, I cursed myself. Just knowing there were people there was the reason I didn't refuse.

I swam to the stern of the tug with two lifeguards.

The boatswain handed us a thin steel line from above. Now, having caught its end to partner with one from the rescuers, we moved quickly down towards the bow of the submarine.

"The shorter I am here, the better for me," I thought as I descended.

We are already with him, at the bottom there are clear marks indicating that the ship has already moved some three meters down.

It was difficult to stay close to the bow of the ship with this current. We strapped a rope to his hull together in a way that makes it immediately detachable in case it goes into the depths unexpectedly.

At the bottom base of the bow there is a special reinforced hole in its plating. This is a place to add a tow. We pass the end of the nib through this eye.

"Up!" I show the rescuer. He grabs the end and quickly emerges past the tug's stern.

After a while, the nib begins to move around the eye. I make sure that it does not become entangled and does not get stuck inside.

I looked up. I can see a thick shackle descending towards us, followed by a thick steel rope - it's from a broken tow. It is already with me. Shit, the spindle is too small! - I think to myself. You need bigger. This one won't cover the eye in the ship. Here you need to translate a pin with a larger diameter.

I looked at my watch. I can leave. I fly up the steel line. I see the boatswain leaning over the water waiting for me. I grab the rope with my left hand and pull off the mask with the other.

"Give me a bigger shackel!" I say to him. "The bigger shackel, the biggest you have!"

"We don't have a bigger one!"

"Then give me five meters of chain. I'll take an eye and wear what's down there. The pulling force will split in half, it's like giving a shackel twice as large," I tell him.

"Okay, I'll leave you in a second," and he headed for the storage. After a while some old piece of thick anchor chain pulled up and started lowering to the bottom. There, together with the lifeguard, we attached it to the nib. I grabbed the nib and tugged it to signal it to pull slowly.

The chain easily passed through the eye in the forward hull of the ship. We connected its two ends to the shackle and the tow was ready.

"I'm going out" I show the rescuers.

"OK" A thumbs up means they understand.

I swam fifty yards away, where a special rope ran from the lifeguards' pontoons down to the hull. Following it, I surfaced very slowly.

When my head was on the surface, Jarek on our pontoon walked towards me. They were waiting for me there - I climbed and said to him:

"Report that they can begin."

Black smoke erupted from the Poseidon's chimney. During this time, the Bo'sun pulled two anchors from the water, keeping the tug in a fixed position. I climbed aboard and went to see the stern. The haul slowly stretched, keeping the ship steady. We'll see in an hour if that helps, I thought and looked up at the sky. Black clouds heralded a change in weather. Not good. During this time, another two sailors landed in our decompression chamber, where immediately they were taken care of by a doctor who doubled and troubled in this cramped room, helping the injured.

Their smiling and happy faces made us feel that our efforts are not in vain. I remembered that I hadn't eaten since breakfast, and that was long after lunch, so I went to the wardroom. As I sat at the table, I saw two helicopters coming from the sea through the porthole. Knowing the situation, the Canadian Command decided that if the rescue vessel could not reach the site yet, helicopters would deliver seamen on it. Better this solution than none. We are running out of space in the chamber. Two more people and no one else will fit. Two places must be in reserve for rescuers. They will also have to go through a decompression chamber if someone - knock on wood - has an accident. Helicopters take turns to secure the evacuation site. One of them froze on the nearby land 300 meters from us. It was an hour and fifteen minutes until the rescue unit arrived. For now, further evacuation of the crew has been suspended. Taking advantage of this, I went to the booth and lay down, I wanted to relax and de-stress. But I had to fall asleep because the boatswain knocked on me saying:

"The rest of the crew from the sunken submarine are already in the decompression chambers of the Canadian rescuer. Come on, you can't miss it. You'll go to sleep later," he says graciously. "After decompression, they are taken by helicopters to Canada," he added.

Three hours after the lifeguard arrived, the Canadian war tug took over the tow from us and all the sailors from our steel monster who served the entire crew. On a submarine six rescuers searched all rooms for living people. I knew that they were no longer there, but I was silent - I don't know why. Our captain has already made a visit on their flagship, collecting praise and congratulations.

We could go on.

# Chapter VII

## Port Naomi

***Canada Wednesday, August 9***

It took us three days to get to the port of destination. What was our surprise when two destroyers greeted us in the roadstead, hitting the blinds with welcoming salvos.

"I guess in our honor!" you can hear the Third.

On the way to the port, we were assisted by a small fire tug, pouring plumes of water from its cannons, and a dozen different boats, yachts, motorboats swirled around him - as if Her Majesty the British Queen had come to the port.

The pilot did not lead us to the quay, where two rusty old ships were waiting for us, but to some representative part of the military wharf.

I was standing on the bridge next to the captain and the boatswain. Jarek and the rest of the crew on board watched in amazement at what was happening.

"You see what I see?" The boatswain asks, his elbow against the porthole, his nose stuck to its glass. "It's good to have the entire ship pimped out."

A dozen or so meters from the quay you can clearly see the crowd of people. There are sailors in the front line in uniforms. Behind them some women, children and some guys going there and back and snapping photos. On the side there is a TV broadcast van, a military orchestra nearby with the conductor waving the lag and waving pirouettes with it around the hand.

"Shit, I didn't expect that," I say.

"And I am," says the captain. "I didn't want to tell you earlier, but I was announced by the head of the company at the invitation of the Canadian Command. There is also a director and a coordinator in sea rescue."

"Well, now there will be panic on the ship," judges the Boss. It was going to be such a nice port. We went out on the wing - immediately people started waving at us and a military brass band started playing.

Once we moored and our gangway hooked for Canadian soil, our captain, who had changed into a representative uniform, came out to meet them.

He ordered us to dress decently and go to the quay.

Everyone waited patiently for our entire crew to stand in front of them. There was not Cook only, who was quickly preparing a welcome snack, because, as Keep rightly stated, a return visit is inevitable.

Where are the Canadian rescuers? I look around but I can't see them. Well, they're the elite, the best of the best, and who were we there? - I wonder. It was only later that I found out that they were still there at the time and were recovering from the ship those crew members who had not survived.

I missed the official speech and a very short military speech.

As I was standing a little to the side, a young woman with two young children approached me. Beautiful, red cloves in her hand were for me.

"Richard! Thank you for saving, for everything," she says, handing me flowers, "and my husband and I invite you to our house!"

"How do you know my name?" I ask. "Whose wife are you?"

I guess she figured out I didn't know who her husband was.

"He's standing there, third from the left," she says.

I'm confused and a little awkward, so I look that way. That's how I recognize him! This is the mechanic in the torpedo compartment, the one in the asbestos blanket, who drew a plan for me to go down to the air cylinder on a piece of paper. I don't even know his name.

She burst out in a soft sob.

"Please don't cry, it's a day of joy!" I try to calm her down.

"These tears are also for joy!" She replies. "I'm Jacqueline, and this is M... and F..." She shows me the two children standing politely by her side. "Gregor will be with us soon."

I thank her for the flowers and she picks up the two little ones in turn and kiss me on the cheek.

I felt faint.

They stand by me and wait for husband to join them. I feel stupid, but I can see that with each of our crew there are even several people at once, because there are many more saved than us.

The orchestra stopped playing and the crowd fell apart, mixed with each other, with us. It was uplifting, a little tender and I felt so uncomfortable somehow.

Jacqueline did not leave Richard one step, and to all who hit him she told them that he was busy and was going to them. Gregor came, approached Ryszard, embraced him and thanked him in sincere words for the rescue.

"Come on, we're going to us. We will be very pleased to get to know you better."

All the while, photojournalists snapped photos and cameras shot the whole spontaneous meeting.

A local TV reporter broke through the families of sailors besieging him.

"We would like to interview you," Ryszard heard the proposal.

"I can't give any interview first. There's a captain there, go see him. But then I serve myself. When I have time, you can see how I am being watched," he said, joking.

"Here, call me," he handed him his card. Canadian families wanted to host us in theirs houses, no other group meeting was planned. It's a very personal event and they are at home while our homes are far away. As they rightly reasoned, private visits would be more important to us. There were few of us, and a lot of them, so each of the Canadian sailors had a point of honor at least once to host one of our crew. We chose rather by profession, that is, the officer who knew English better directed our sailors to similar maritime specialties.

Ryszard was the most recognizable member of the tug's crew. Although he did not record - except three - no other faces, he was seen by all the seamen of the submarine. The same was true of Third and Jarek, because of their supervision over the decompression of the ship's crew, which they were initially involved in.

Gregor's wife - a tall young woman - had black, long hair, and the features of her face were telling about the fact that there is an admixture of different blood in it, maybe Indian, but Ryszard was not sure, and he wasn't going to ask. She was pretty, shapely, and didn't look as mother of two small children who stood next to him, holding hands.

The two toddlers looked shyly at Ryszard. The girl, maybe seven or eight years old, was bolder and spoke to him something. He couldn't hear her because every now and then someone wanted to kidnap him with him. The constant "Sorry, but I've got an appointment" was starting to piss him off. The orchestra played again and there was a lot of noise around and loud conversations.

"What's your name?" He asked, turning to the girl who stood beside her, holding her mother's hand. Jacqueline tried to isolate the children and Ryszard from the rest of the besieging guests. The girl cannot hear him. He looks at Ryszard as if he were some painting.

"What's up?" he thought.

He crouched down beside her and said:

"I'm Richard, and you?"

"M..., and this is K..., my brother, but he is afraid of everything."

"Me too?"

"No, not you. Mom said you were an angel." Jacqueline, hearing what M... says, cuts in:

"Yes, it's true," she confirms. "I said it might.

Be some angel who brought you to them."

"You know who a cetacean is, a whale?" Ryszard asked.

"I know, they are such big fish, sometimes you can see them from our house, affecting the bay."

"They were what led us to your dad." They both looked at him in disbelief.

But he was not allowed to tell them now how they ended up in a submarine.

The captain called the entire crew to the wardroom.

"Wait ten minutes, it won't take longer," Ryszard said to them, nervous about the unexpected pause. He liked the offer to visit their home. This is because of the special reception they prepared for him, as well as the plan that began to sprout in his head.

"Relax, take your time. We will wait for how much it will have to."

He went on the tug, to the wardroom. Everyone's already were there.

A short thank you for the successful rescue operation was given to them by the company boss, and the captain ended the meeting by saying:

"You have two days off, it's a bonus from the management. Only the watch remains. I think Cook also deserves days off. Will you be able to cook yourselves?" He asked.

"Sure, no problem. The watch will serve itself," you can hear the voice of the boatswain, although he is not currently keeping watch.

"Good - there are four people left. Watches six by six. Set it up with yourselves. People who leave the city enter the phone number and the address where they are going into the book.

Only, gentlemen - no fooling around. We have a good record and let it stay that way. Understand?" He finished.

There were voices of satisfaction. Ryszard calmly changed his clothes, put a few more essentials in his bag and went to the Lieutenant McLanger's family waiting for him.

They waited under the gangplank. Gregor entered the telephone number and address in the book which, on the table by the gangplank, was the busiest place on the quay. Then he and his wife took Ryszard in the middle and together they went to the exit gate.

Imagine his surprise when he was allowed through without any formalities, and a seaman standing on watch saluted him.

"How does he know me?" He wondered.

In the parking lot, they got into the large Land Rover and headed towards the city in sight.

"Richard, Richard!" little M... pulls him by the sleeve. "Where do you live?" She asks, looking at him curiously.

"In Poland."

"It is far?"

"By plane several hours."

"Well, not far then," she said pleased. They were just approaching a hill covered with houses.

They were all similar to each other, clinging to the entire hilly area. With one of them, Jacqueline, because she was driving the car, stopped with the words:

"We're in the place."

They went inside. Ryszard looked inside the living room curiously. Nice, cozy and quite a lot of space for such a family, his unfinished house crossed his mind.

This one also had an attic, but now there were two kids who wanted to show off their treasures to the "angel". M... dragged a big doll down saying:

"This is Mary, whom I love very much and she doesn't like me leaving her alone."

I think they have already accepted him, because right behind his sister little K... put a robot on his lap.

"You can play," he said, and after a moment's thought he added, "But only a little."

Jacqueline was preparing dinner at the time at the far end of the lounge where there was a kitchenette.

"Just like mine," Ryszard was amazed.

"So what was it like with those whales?" She called to him from a distance. At that time, Gregor was lighting a fire in the fireplace. Then, without waiting for her answer, he pulled out a Scotch whiskey and asked:

"What are we drinking? Maybe you prefer pure vodka?"

"No thanks. Whiskey will be fine."

Without being on the subject, she looks towards wives.

"What whales are you talking about?"

Richard sighed and looked up to the wide windows overlooking the bay. He got up and walked over to that glass wall.

"Gregor, M... she said you can see blue whales from here."

"Yes, we watched them with the children many times," Jacqueline cut in, hugging Gregor lovingly. With her other hand she handed Ryszard a glass with whiskey.

"Have you ever wondered that they are watching you too?"

He saw their exchange of glances.

"No, we didn't think of it," she said, slightly surprised. She looked at him, not really knowing what he was going to. "It's just a fish, only big one. What could she be watching?" Her eyes seem to tell this.

"But it has to be likethat. They are extremely intelligent, they can think like people and have feelings."

Now it exaggerates, she thought, but she was tactfully silent, not wanting to offend him.

"What I am going to tell you seems unbelievable to me, but it was so, and the best proof of it is the fact that I am here with you."

They both sat on the couch, and Ryszard crashed into the armchair. Although several days have passed since these events, he had them before his eyes as if it were yesterday.

When he finished telling how "Poseidon" dropped the anchor and he went down into the water and saw their ship at the bottom - he realized that he was right. They wouldn't be here together if it weren't for the whales.

"Gregor, do you have any explanation for their behavior?" Ryszard asked, looking in amazement at the bottom of his glass. "When did I drink it?"

Gregor got up and poured again, and after they had all drank, they moved to a large table covered with tasty delicacies, which emanated the irritating smell of roast turkey.

Sitting at the table made it easier to speak about painful things. However, nobody raised this issue, they circled the subject, but so far it had been a taboo, the line of which they were afraid to cross.

"Okay. I will tell you what I think about it," said Ryszard, who was disturbed by the blue whale issue. "I think they treated the ship as their individual and wanted to help him. Hence their actions.

It was too shallow for them there, so they looked for an ally and turned to us, directing our tug to the right place.

"No... They knew very well that there were people who needed help," said Gregor, who had been silent until now.

"How did they know?" Surprised Jacqueline stopped her hand over the plate.

"From us?" Now Ryszard froze with curiosity.

"We speak their language," Gregor finally choked out. "But this is a military secret... Maybe not entirely, but not everyone knows that their singing can be imitated and we did just that. No matter why or for what purpose, it's so confusingly similar that some whales fall for it... Not to mention humans.

"This only confirms the assumption that they are very intelligent and caring, if they wanted to help you."

Time passed quickly on their talks. They did not come back to the subject of the disaster. All evening Ryszard was choked with wanting to tell Gregor about his suspicions about the "poppy field," as he called it, something near their ship. However, he wanted to better prepare for this conversation. He still had to check on the Internet to see if his suspicions were right and if that was what he was thinking about all the time.

"When do you have to get back to the ship?" Jacqueline's question tore him out from reflection.

"I don't have to go back. My alternate arrives tomorrow morning and I return to my home country. My contract is over."

And they ran out of Scotch whiskey. Gregor took out another one, but Ryszard drew alcohol from it very slowly, not wanting to exceed his abilities.

"Stay with us for a while. We will show you the city, the surrounding area, we will go fishing. No! Better not to fish," Gregor corrected immediately.

Jacqueline showed Ryszard his room. Upstairs, next to the kids, comfortable and non-binding room with bathroom for guests.

"When you have enough of us, feel free to go upstairs to sleep," she added.

Immediately afterwards she asked: "Stay with us for a while. Help Gregor, he was just talking about you the whole time. Something's bothering him, but he won't talk to me about it. Not with a psychologist either. "Only Richard can explain it to me," he told me one evening. "I have to find him, even if I'm going to go to Poland." We did not know yet that you would be here," she explains at the end.

I thought for a moment. What should I explain to him? - I couldn't remember anything like that.

Then there were a lot of photos from family albums, and what next - I don't really remember. However, I went up alone.

In the morning, or actually almost noon, I am tired with an amazing hangover. Quick shower, toilet, clean clothes, and I land at Jacqueline's in the kitchen. She greets me as if we haven't seen each other for a hundred years and we knew each other twice as much.

"You want coffee," she says rather than asks as she pushes a cup under the coffee machine.

I pour the milk myself and then help her set the table. A huge table stands by the window in the kitchenette and is only used for breakfast, Jacqueline explains to me.

"Then when M... goes to school and K... goes to kindergarten. We eat lunch at home and then dinner at home. Of course, as Gregor is with us and not at sea. I'm already used to his cruises into the unknown. I never know when, where or how long he will be gone. Not like you," she says with a slight envy in her voice. "You do the contract and come back."

"I'm going back, yes, but to the empty walls."

"Don't worry, it will change soon. It's impossible for a guy like you not to find a girlfriend," she comforts me.

We eat a typical American breakfast - cereal with milk, eggs and bacon and toasts.

Gregor isn't here yet.

"He's still asleep," says Jacqueline.

"I have to go to the ship, probably the alternate man is already there," I explain.

"My sister will take you. She will wait there and bring you back. I would give you a car, but you still have too much alcohol in you," she smiles at me.

"Are you sure you want me back?" I ask just in case.

"Of course! I wouldn't let you go anywhere anyway." She came up to me, hugged me like a brother and said:

"Come back, please."

"What about my visa?"

"I'll get it right away," she promised.

"OK. I will be there as soon as possible."

I was finishing my coffee when the girl entered the lounge.

"I'm Keys," she says, and walks over to me, her greenish eyes piercing at me. She wasn't super beautiful, but she had that "something", as if the Petty Officer had said. The complete opposite of Jacqueline. Of medium height, with a pretty face and green eyes, plus thick auburn hair in a bun showing her long, shapely neck. In a nice, slightly hoarse voice, she said, turning to me:

"I'm completely at your disposal. This is the Richard." Keys looked at him sideways. She had expected a sailor's weathered face, like in those short, not very clear films on TV. And here is a tall, handsome guy standing in front of her with dark hair and a youthful face, his brown eyes staring at her curiously. She was looking at that nice, smiling face of a young boy, and yet she knew that he would turn thirty soon. When they showed him and Jarek on television, briefly describing their biographies and saying that now the lives of all the sailors from their sunken submarine depend on these two rescuers from the Polish tug "Poseidon", she thought:

"How will they handle it?"

Then all of Canada was relieved to see the diver connects them with life-giving air, and Ryszard enters the ship. These short videos from their underwater camera, probably sent somewhat illegally by someone from a warship, were watched with excitement by millions of Canadians.

In the studio, experts announced that the chances of survival of the remaining sailors in compartment IV are minimal, and their air has run out or is about to end, making all their relatives despair with this statement. Oxygen cannot be supplied to them from outside, and access to them from the battle conning tower where Ryszard entered is impossible.

After half an hour, the whole of Canada gasped, seeing him enter the 4th compartment through the third torpedo tube, and Jarek, standing by him, protects him. Two hours of tension passed before they saw him again. In fact, they only saw him for a brief moment, coming out of the water onto the deck of the Poseidon. They saw his very tired face with blue, dark circles under his eyes. Then a crazy burst of joy as their captain gave the news that thirty-eight sailors were alive and that they would be saved. How he did it - they didn't know until they heard it from Gregor.

"This is my little sister," comes Jacqueline's voice. "Do you want some coffee?" She asks.

"No, thank you," she says, still staring at me.

"This declaration of yours is dangerous," I joke, addressing Keys. I get up, we shake hands, and I offer her a chair for her to sit down.

She looked at me, understanding nothing. This is what it is with the American, you speak Polish while thinking, and it comes not what you want.

"It's such a word play," I explain to Keys the meaning of the sentence. But she didn't understand anyway because she said:

"More than one girl would like to show you the city. And show with you," she adds.

"And you?" I ask. "What would you show me?"

"Anything you want," she replies. "I'm free. We can go sightseeing, watch, go to a disco, drink a little..."

I'd like to see you, I thought, but I kept my mouth shut. She wouldn't understand this joke and there will be an affront.

"Will you stay with us longer?" She asks.

"I will stay, I have a business to do."

Jacqueline looked at me surprised. Then she smiled happily. She probably thought I meant Gregor, but she was wrong.

"Then we have an appointment. I'll come pick you up on Friday after work," she sealed the brief exchange. Probably each of us understood it differently. Oh, never mind. I like discos and the atmosphere there - I think.

"OK," I answer.

"Thanks, Jacqueline," she said to her sister.

The coffee is drunk, so we go with Keys to the car.

"Do you have a phone?" She asked before she left the house.

"I have."

"Give me it," she asked.

I handed her my cell phone. She took my card out of it and inserted a local one, then tapped some numbers.

"Now we can keep in touch. You have a number for Gregor, Jacqueline, and me there."

"Thanks, you've thought of everything," I praise her. All the way she told me about herself: about work, about the neighborhood and that she likes karaoke.

They let us in through the main gate and Keys pulled up to the very gangway of Poseidon.

"Do you want to come in?" I ask.

"Not today, thanks. Call me when you're ready. I will pick you up."

"Fine," I said, and she drove off.

Tadek, my substitute, was waiting in the wardroom. I quickly handed over my duties to him, packed my bag and suitcase, dumped everything on the deck and ...was free.

The captain was gone, nobody was there, I don't even have anyone to say goodbye to. But I'm not flying home today, so I'll be there in a few days.

From the Office I called the office in Gdynia.

"I'm not going to Poland tomorrow," I informed Ms Ula. "I am re-booking my tickets and let you know when I get back."

"Congratulations, Mr. Richard. And have a nice vacation," I only hear.

It's my private business, what I do after the contract, but she knows I'm calling to let her know I'm not coming on that plane. That's right. I sat down with the boys for a while, we looked at today's newspapers full of reports from the past days. I read our Old Man's interview, told them I was staying in Canada for a few days, and called Keys.

"I'm on my way," I heard.

Of course, everyone who was on the ship went out to see who had come for me.

Keys got to the gangplank and got out from the car and leaning on the hood, she was waiting for me. There was a lot of appropriate oohs and ahs, but nothing she hear was vulgar.

She blushed, I said in amazement, looking at the smile of satisfaction at the compliments flying in her direction.

Tadek helped me put my modest luggage in the car and I left with Keys.

"What about my visa?" I asked, already sitting in the car.

"I just got a call from Jacqueline. The visa is cleared, it will be ready tomorrow. The Navy Command made an effort and you don't even have to bother with them. You are on the VIP List of Honorary Guests. As long as you like."

At my request, we went into the city, to some shopping center, where I did some shopping for myself and picked up some cash from an ATM.

"Keys, tomorrow Friday. Before you show me how you have fun, please take me to some diving club, it can be private or otherwise. I guess you have something like that here?"

"We have the "Naomi Diving Club" here, they even have their own vessel for sailing on the sea."

I looked at her face as we walked downtown. It was obvious that she was pleased when someone stopped us. In fact, some people kept addressing me greetings.

We had to stop twice, because we came across families of sailors who really wanted to exchange a few words with me.

Nice, although for me the same words, gestures and thanks were tiring. As we walked back to the car, Keys grabbed my hand and pulled me across the parking lot.

What happened to her? - I wondered about her behavior.

"Come on, faster! This is the wife of one of the sailors who died."

But it didn't help - after a while a young girl stood in our way. Tall, slender blonde with her face swollen from crying.

"You're Richard," she said.

"Glass, come on, don't bother him."

"You know they won't tell me anything," she turned sad eyes to Keys. "I have to ask him, I have to! Only he can tell me that."

There was nothing good for me in this exchange of views. I realized Keys was trying to protect me from something. I see Glass pull out a photo and Keys freed hands holding the girl.

She wasn't pushy or harassing me. She was sad, very sad, and this sadness was tearing out of her whole character.

"Have you seen him, Richard?" She asked.

I took the photo from her hand and recognized him immediately. It's the young boy I grabbed by the belt. I had to visibly change my face because she quietly said:

"You saw Jonathan..."

Keys grabbed my hand. I squeezed her unconsciously.

"Yes, I did," I said softly. "When I got to him, he was already dead."

"He suffered?" She just asked.

"No, definitely not," he wasn't burned. He fell asleep. He had your photo in his hand," I lied. I don't know why I said that, I wanted to ease her suffering.

She burst into loud crying and walked away in a small step.

"I need a drink," I just said. "That's the other side of the coin," I added, looking at Keys. "Come on for a drink."

"Sorry, someone must have told her you are here."

"Don't apologize, it's not you who are to blame, it's a WWII mine."

"What?!" She blurted out unexpectedly. "They said nothing about any of the mine!"

"Bloody hell!" I cursed. Keep it to yourself, I don't want to spread unofficial versions of the accident that happened to this ship here.

We entered some bar where I drank a hundred milliliter strong Russian vodka. And not only because we met Glass, but also because the hangover was so bad for me.

On the way to the Diving Club, Keys confided in me, surprising me with the topic:

"Almost two years ago I broke up with my boyfriend who was on this ship. This is Gregor's friend. He did not survive the accident, so I wanted to get to know you so much. I asked Jacqueline to arrange this. Don't be angry with me, but I wanted to ask you the same question Glass did. I cured myself from love to him a long time ago because he hurt me a lot then. But I would sleep calmer if I knew what Glass knows."

I was silent, what was I supposed to say to her? If only I would not regret staying here, I thought, surprised by what happened to me.

"When Gregor came home, he only talked about you, but nothing specific."

"What was he saying?" I asked.

"That he needs to talk to you, but what about, he didn't want to say. The only time, Jacqueline was gone, he said to me:

'I saw something - it was about Richard, that's why we're alive.' And then he seemed scared of what he said to me, because he added, 'I must have imagined it.' We know nothing more, do you understand any of this?" She asked.

"I think so, but this conversation is not for now."

She paused for a long moment, concentrating on the road, which meandered in gentle hairpin turns, leading us down to the marina.

"Should I go with you?" She asked when we got there.

"I'm asking you to do this, I will be more credible when I talk to them."

We stood next to a small, white, nicely finished one-story building with a huge inscription "Naomi Diving Club" crowned with a logo - a diving helmet woven into the anchor.

"Their ship is there," said Keys, pointing to a converted fishing boat, aged but well-kept.

We go inside. On the left a warehouse, where through the open door you can see hanging suits and other diving equipment. On the right side the door with the word "Office".

I knock and walk in - there's an old guy sitting at desk in front of me, maybe a bit in his sixties, and something is tapping the computer with one finger.

He looked at us bored, sullenly. Seeing me, he sprang up violently to meet us.

"You're that Richard," he said in a surprised voice. This time, I didn't mind that he recognized me.

"I think so, if you mean the guy from the Polish tug Poseidon," I introduced myself in an unusual way.

"I'm Bill," he introduced himself. "The boss of this club. Keys, what are you doing here? Please sit down." He moved two dilapidated chairs towards us.

"Do you all know each other?" I asked Keys.

"Almost everyone. It's a small town," she replied, laughing at my puzzled expression.

"Congratulations, Richard. Your entry through the launcher into the ship was a masterpiece. You surprised everyone."

"Thanks, Bill."

"What brings you to me?"

"An important matter, very important to me. This personal, unusual request. I would like to penetrate one spot near the one where your submarine crashed. For this I need equipment: a ship that would drop me off there and help with the protection of two or three experienced divers.

"What depths are you talking about?" expertly asks about the most important aspect of each dive.

"Up to forty meters, no more."

"It can be done," he said. "It's a wreck?"

"No, not a wreck, a rock cleft. I don't know what's behind it. You are the first person I tell about this to and let it stay that way," I'm asking him.

"Sure, it's your assignment. What else?" he asks.

"I don't have anything here, so pretty much everything. For this some light, power generator, bottom signals, safety lines. Two or three buoys, some food."

"It can be done," he repeated, curious about what he heard.

"Oh, and definitely a satellite phone. And if you have it, it's an underwater camera. If you don't have it, I'll buy it."

"I have everything except the underwater camera. Something else?"

"That's it," I sighed heavily, thinking about the fact that now it's time to move on to finance. Will my pocket stand it? - I wonder.

He could feel that sigh as he smiled from under his bushy mustache.

"How much do you value your services?" I ask.

"Not so fast, Richard. I need to talk to the guys, then I'll let you know. When do you want to go?"

"If the weather forecast will be good, but as soon as possible, because I'm a guest at McLanger's."

"Keys, what are you going to do there?" He asked.

"I can cook you if Richard asks me for this trip."

I turned my head towards her in surprise.

"You want to come with us?"

"Very much!"

"If so, that's fine," I said to Keys.

"Another person will come with us, I haven't talked to her about it yet. I'll let you know when I know."

I talked a little more about the equipment they have and the possibilities of their ship. Everything was modern, efficient and with approvals. The divers and scuba divers with diplomas and extensive experience. The decompression chamber is roomy enough.

We made an appointment for Monday.

"Looking forward to hearing from you, Bill. Call me," I say goodbye.

"No, no! We'll all meet here and discuss the details. You will see the equipment, visit the ship, prepare cameras and everything you need, most importantly, you will meet the guys and maybe even one of the girls."

"Bill... I don't know if I can afford such a trip," I say bluntly, not mince matters. "Better call us sooner and give the price, so that there will be no disappointments."

"Don't worry, we'll handle it." Satisfied with his declaration, I caught it unknowingly Keys by the hand and after saying goodbye, we went outside. She held my hand to the car itself. She had nice velvety skin with long fingers and long nails as well. Hope it's artificial."

"Keys, what did you think about this trip?"

"I like adventure and I have been diving with them several times. But I don't dive," she enlightens me immediately.

We return to Jacqueline, from where Keys disappears after an hour to work.

"I would like to stay with you! But I have to go to work," she says. "I'll come by tonight. I'll get the beer. Do you like?" She asks.

"Sure I do, but take the local ones, not some known brands," I laugh.

Tomorrow's Friday. I was supposed to go with Keys to the disco, but I don't think it'll succeed, because Jacqueline announced a big family gathering on Friday afternoon.

It's cold outside for me, but it's the middle of summer here, so they took advantage of the opportunity to do a great barbecue outside. The whole family and a few friends with their wives and kids came. I took Jarek and the boatswain, as representatives of the crew, from "Poseidon". These are their last days in port - they are going to Egypt soon.

The fun was gaining momentum. The music was playing, the smoke carried the smells from the grill, and punch and something stronger were at hand. I was sitting with Keys, sipping local beer and told her about Sopot, where I live and what I do when I am off. I've decided to talk to Gregor now. He probably wouldn't have started this conversation himself, I thought, looking at him. Seemingly calm, cheerful, he honors the host, but I know that inside he is consumed with anxiety and uncertainty as to whether he is all right.

I like Keys more and more, not only because she clings to me.

Had she taken her sister's words to heart so much?

"Take care of Richard, he's very lonely here and in his country too," he jokes. "He told me about it himself," he adds, winking at Keys.

Shit, and I don't remember anything about this talk. But it probably was, when I drank, I complained to her.

I take Gregor aside and say to him:

"Come on, let's talk."

He was a little scared that this would soon turn out to be what he feared very much. Conversations about those moments.

"You saw her," I shoot blindly as we walked away from everyone and sat on the fallen trunks of old trees.

His eyes grew round as big coins, and his chin began to tremble.

"You too?" He asked.

"Yes, several times."

"How is this possible?"

"I don't know, and I don't care." Out of the corner of my eye I see Jacqueline and Keys watch us anxiously, guessing what we are doing in private.

"She's a friendly soul, she helps me. Tell me what did you see?"

"When you knocked the S.O.S. into the flap of the launcher, we had hope of rescue. However, there was a technical problem. Those launchers with closed flaps gave no chance of getting inside. The explosion blocked all hydraulic connections. Only in this one, not because they were in the unlocked position. However, it was necessary to enter the room with the launcher's maneuvering levers and switch the valve to manual maneuvers. There was water, cold water, and it was dark. It was my job, but I was afraid, and I was also afraid to do nothing, because it meant certain death. As I was standing over the hatch with one of my colleagues standing next to me, I saw a greenish figure of a woman. She waved in the water at me, urging me to come in. I was even more scared. I called to my friend if he could see anything in the water and he replied that he couldn't see anything and that I was hallucinating from oxygen deficiency. I thought so then too. When I dipped up to my neck, she was gone. Shivering from cold, I swam the few meters under the water. I quickly dealt with the shifting of the valve and when submerged in this cold water I returned to the hatch, and my lungs screamed for air, I saw her again. She was standing outside and smiling at me. Chills shook my whole body, I didn't know if it was from cold or lack of oxygen. I asked my friend again if there was anyone around him. He didn't even bother to take off his mask to deny it. He just shook his head. Then two others went to get you and I rested in the corner. When I went with you to the companionway to the engine room, and you were going down to the water, I saw it again, but this time it was not facing me, it was in yours. I thought you saw her too - she was standing in front of you. You kept your eyes on it, shining the light from your flashlight on it. You raised your hand in a gesture of welcome, then plunged into the water, disappearing into the darkness.".

"Yes, she was there for a while," I admitted to him.

Relief crossed his face.

He wasn't crazy and he didn't think anything.

"But don't boast about it to anyone," I add. "SHE wishes so. I don't know why it appeared to you, there must be some reason. Maybe it is just for you to help me."

"In what?"

"I have some suspicions about the place where the shipwreck occurred."

I described to him a poppy field and a large hole in the rock.

"I don't know what it is, but it is definitely related to this rock cleft."

"We need to talk to Big Ear," he said. "If it's any underwater device, he'll know what it is."

"There's something else. Almost in front of this gap, on land, was once a settlement of whalers. Nothing survived there except the skeletons of whales and the crumbling cabin boards. I checked on the Internet. In 1918, there were German explorers in this settlement interested in whaling. None of these catches have worked out, but maybe there is something to do with all of this."

"I don't know... I'll check if it's marked on military maps."

"No better not. Let that stay between us until we figure out what we're dealing with. I made contact with the local Diving Club. I will see what is behind it. Swim with me! If you've seen her, she probably wants you there."

He looked at me suspiciously. I spoke of the Apparition as if it were a living being. He couldn't believe it.

One thing is "apparition" under stress and the lack of oxygen, and a other thing is garden, barbecue and beer - how to reconcile it? - his face told me.

I patted him on the back.

"I'm surprised by everything, but the fact that the whales led us to you is also unbelievable as what you saw."

"Yes you are right. I will go," he said confidently. "You were with me, and now I'll be with you."

We finished the topic and returned to the guests.

After a while, Jacqueline sent me a charming smile of satisfaction, and Keys a long-distance kiss.

Jarek was the leader among girls, and the boatswain with his inseparable Cuba Libra in his hand, he caused volleys of laughter, telling stories from the life of sailors. I spent the rest of my time with Keys.

Well after midnight, she asked:

"Walk me home, it's close."

"Okay, I'd love to, but how do I get back?" I asked. "What if I get lost?"

"Would you get lost? No, it's impossible," she teases me.

On the way, she tells me that Gregor has come back to life after our conversation.

"He told Jacqueline that he was fine and was alright. He seduced her all evening afterward. They haven't slept together since he got back. It worried her a lot, now she won't let her sleep for sure," she talks to me, a little drunk.

"What's her point? Maybe she wants me to do do the same?"

I think to myself.

"Do you want to see how I live?" She asked when we got to her house.

"Do you have drip coffee?"

"I have something better," she laughed and kissed me unexpectedly on the lips.

I stayed until noon.

"You have the keys and take the car, I will go to work with my friend, I've already talked to her."

"What about Jacqueline and Gregor?" I ask, slightly confused.

"You're an adult, and so am I. For now, I have to go. I'll see you at noon."

"I don't even know where you work!" I threw for her.

"I have a boutique in the mall," she says at the door.

I spent the entire Saturday and Sunday with McLangers and the kids. Keys took a break from work and spent part of the day with us. She and Jacqueline kept talking about me behind my back when they thought I couldn't see it. But no word was said about my late night visits to Keys and my early return to them.

I was their guest and - as it turned out - a guest of Keys. They showed me the neighborhood, some kind of City Museum and a national park with numerous natural attractions. Time passed quickly. I felt very well with them, but knew that this visit should now be completed and go back to what I stayed here for. They realized my presence it is also related to my trip.

# Chapter VIII

# Whalers Cave

*Monday, August 14*

We leave on Thursday. Bill called on Monday morning.

"I agreed with the guys that you will pay the fuel costs. The rest is exercise and pleasure. A food dump and we can go. Come in this afternoon, they really want to meet you and find out more details."

"Okay, I'll be there at seven."

I had something else to do.

"You know what?" Jacqueline tells me over coffee as I introduce Gregor to my conversation with Bill. "Do you remember that reporter? He wants an interview, and you have an ace up your sleeve. They will definitely be interested in your exclusive proposition from this escapade, and maybe even send a reporter with a camera with you. If you come across something, you sell them the rights to the report."

"Interesting thought. But I don't feel strong enough to negotiate it with them."

"You don't have to, remember when William offered his help on the grill if you needed anything?"

"I remember, but it's just polite talk."

"No, he is a lawyer, he has his own law office. If you agree, I'll call him. He will represent you."

"Jacqueline, you're nice, but it costs money too. I don't know if I can afford it. I heard the lawyers in Canada, they start operating at $10,000. It's not for me."

"Maybe they take that much, but if you find something, he will earn a commission from TV, and if not, he will do it for free for you, for us."

I had nothing to lose. And only to gain.

"Okay, call him."

At noon, at lunchtime, Keys drove up to us. She greeted everyone and gave me a kiss in my mouth.

"How did you sleep?" She asked perversely. She left early in the morning before I woke up.

"I wasn't sleeping at all, I was too stuffy," I say, alluding to her nightly games.

"I took a vacation from today, the girls will help me and I will help you in organizing the trip," she says excitedly.

"Gregor, get some maps of this area. They may be old, but accurate," I'm asking him.

Jacqueline just came back from the other room saying:

"You've got an appointment. Keys, Richard and you will go to William's office, I've already made an appointment for five o'clock. Go with them to talk to TV tomorrow, he'll feel better."

"Did you call there too?" I ask surprised.

"Of course, it's easier for me to talk to them. They were surprised, they thought you were already in Poland. But they are still very interested. When I told them you do some mysterious case, they crowed with delight. 'We're in,' said their program director."

"Are you not my manager?" Satisfied, I laugh at her actions.

We drove from Keys to William, he's some distant cousin of hers. I did not know their family connections, I did not care, I was heading towards my goal and that was all that mattered.

Satisfied with the course of the conversation, I relied entirely on him. I signed a relevant power of attorney and consent to a 15% commission on future income.

"It's insanely low, usually it is 30%," Keys convinces me. "You are lucky, they never give up on higher earnings unless they have a good deal. I guess it is with you anyway."

I invited Keys, Gregor and Jacqueline to the Northern lights restaurant for the evening dinner. I would like to thank them for their care with which they took care of me and my problems. This place was recommended to me by the expert of the subject, my neighbor Jacqueline, during the famous barbecue.

I chose it because you could also dance there, and Tuesday is karaoke day. The disco didn't work out, so maybe we'll dance here before our trip.

I call before lunch and ask for a Tuesday reservation for four.

"There are no vacancies," I hear a nice voice. "Find out tomorrow, maybe someone will refuse the reservation."

"And I have already invited them there - now what?" - I think. The next day, when Keys went to work, I drove her car to the place. By the way, I'll find out more," I thought.

The city center on the promenade.

The magnificent building houses the "Northern lights".

I walk in, slightly surprised by the elegance and glitz of the place. As standard, at the entrance, the manager of the hall greets me, inviting me inside.

When I reveal the purpose of my visit to him, he is surprised that I have bothered myself.

"It was enough to call, I don't have a reservation list," he explains and leads me to some place manager.

Before I could present what brought me to them, the latter, seeing me, called out to the whole room:

"It's Richard! I'm so glad you visited us! Sit down, how can I help you?"

I explain what it is about.

"No problem, you have the table. We are glad that you will be our guest."

So in the evening we all pimped up at our table. On this occasion, I bought a whole layette, because no one takes formal suits and the rest with them on a contract.

The music played and we ordered Canadian specials. I rely entirely on Keys.

"Order me something regional that will surprise me," I asked. "And it's not easy to surprise a sailor who has traveled around the world a few times," I laughed when she asked what I liked.

We spent our time eating good, we danced quite a lot, Keys sang and the drunk vodka buzzed in our heads when in the morning we decided to leave the place. I called the waiter and asked for the bill.

Instead of the bill, the manager of the hall came up.

"Are you satisfied? The food tasted?" He asked.

We praise food and music very much. It was nice.

I hand him my ATM card.

"Thank you," he says. "But the bill already paid. We all looked at him and then at each other."

"Did any of you pay? - I asked.

"No!" All three shake their heads.

"Who paid?" I ask the manager.

"I don't know," he says, and walks off to the next client.

I shrug my shoulders.

"I'll find out later," I tell them, and we go to the taxi. Me with Keys to separate.

As I found out later from their manager, one of the customers across the room paid. Some grayish older man. But who it was, they never told me.

"Richard, I can't tell you that, he's our regular customer. I promised to be silent. All I can tell you is that when he paid he said to me, 'I owe him a debt of gratitude for saving my son'."

In the late afternoon we sat down for a conference. Gregor, Bill, Keys and the seaman he invited, the boatswain Big Ear. You have to reveal cards - at least some of them.

"Tell me what it could be," I tell them about the "poppy field" and describe what I saw there.

Of course, without information about the Almond Apparition.

Nobody can say anything about this strange creation of the human hand.

Gregor unfolds the maps and photos of the settlement that he brought. Somewhere in the archive he dug up photos from 1934, when the settlement was still teeming with life in the summer. No one lived there permanently, but whalers used it.

He placed them next to the current photos taken a few years ago.

Then we marked the position of the rock breach on this map. Keys had drawn a "poppy field", a chasm and a steeply sloping bottom on its sea side.

"Interesting," said the Petty Officer.

"Speak!" Gregor urged him. He was a mechanic himself, not very familiar with the intricacies of navigation charts. Bill also saw nothing and had no associations, although he knew the maps.

Me and the boatswain were trying to figure out what it could be, and nothing occurred to us. It probably would have stayed that way if it weren't for Keys.

"Look at the photos!" She said suddenly.

"So what? I can't see anything, only the stones and the remains of the hut," I say.

"No, not here. Here, a little further, more to the right." We all look, but see nothing. Keys can't stands it and picks up the pencil. Draws an ellipse around the stones in the photos from 1995. They are arranged next to each other, forming two parallel lines.

"And now look here," she is giving us photos from 1934. Indeed - these stones are not there.

"And what does that show?" Bill asks.

"About someone who placed these stones on purpose after 1934."

"Okay, maybe you're right, but for what purpose?"

"I know what," in a whisper, magnifying our surprise, says the boatswain Big Ear.

He takes two clearer photos with stones and puts them on our map.

Our faces must have been astonished, because Jacqueline, entering the living room, asked:

"What were you running into? You look like you've discovered something important."

"Because it is!" the boatswain responds. The path drawn by Keys through the "poppy field" perfectly coincided with the one drawn by the stones in the photos.

"Maybe it's a bearing for ships," he says. "Signpost to the anchorage."

"They didn't need that. Even in 34, they knew how to use better ways to get where they intended," Bill explains to them. "Besides, that doesn't explain the point of putting a "poppy field" there."

"Navigators may not be, but..." Big Ear thinks hard, staring at the photos and Keys drawing.

"This is for a submarine that lines up along these stones and then dives to the correct depth."

"For what?" I ask.

"I do not know yet. Unless there is a chasm to contain such a ship. Then these pots are a signpost for leading the submerged ship. The depth can be quite accurately controlled, but they deviated to the left and right at the same current as there - not much. When the ship deviates from the selected course, the tanks pound against the hull letting you know that the course needs to be improved. That's the only reasonable explanation," he finishes, glad to have solved the mystery.

"Is that our navy," Gregor asks.

"Certainly not yours or anyone's. Nobody's anymore. The pots are old, as old as that mine," I tell them.

"Germany?" Keys asks.

"Yes you are right. I think the German Navy had its base there."

"But where? There's nothing on land there," Gregor wonders.

"Now it may not be. Though I'm not so sure. But maybe it used to be. In 1918, there was a German research expedition there, maybe they discovered something."

"Richard... You know what the sensation would be if you found out you're right?" Jacqueline says.

"I know, but no one can find out about it, because we will not be allowed to look there."

"Sure, you're right! Not a word to anyone," Bill is excited and backing me up.

"William's calling. He asks if we can fit two more people on the ship. The cameraman and the reporter want to keep an eye on you," Jacqueline is standing against the doorframe, receiver in hand, waiting for an answer.

I looked at Bill.

"Let them go, cover the cost of the fuel. The place is enough."

*Thursday, August 17*

We're leaving this morning.

Keys yesterday finished supplying Bill's ship, gracefully called "Medusa", and Bill himself had stitched everything up. We waited for the TV people and Jacqueline and the children were standing next to the quay.

When the car with the word TV pulled up, the local reporter turned out to be a young woman, and the cameraman was an even younger man. They lugged their gear onto the ship and we bounced off the quay without too much goodbye.

Medusa's crew was his Captain Bill, one motorcyclist and two sailors, then three divers, including one woman, me, Gregor, Keys, and two from TV - twelve in all. Except for the captain, they all had double cabins.

There were seven cabins in total, so I chose one with Keys. Two girls with each other and all the rest to their liking.

"Can you cook? It's a whole army of mouths to eat," I tease Keys. "You won't have time for me at all."

But the captain gave the crew no illusions.

"It's not a trip," he said. He assigned duties in the kitchen, people responsible for the order and cleanliness of the rooms, and gave me one watch in a day.

"It would be a sin not to take advantage of you," he said.

I didn't argue at all - it's only four hours. And three days' journey will pass quickly. The weather was relatively good. Only a cold wind was blowing from the north. After working hours, we mainly dealt with talking.

"Why are we going there?" they asked unoriented. The captain cut off all speculation by saying:

"Even if you strain your brains, you will not guess. We are to practice diving in difficult sea current conditions. That must be enough for now."

The TV crew recorded the most interesting moments of our lives on this ship groaning that it was boring and wasted time, and they do not even know why the boss told them to come with us. They were not even aware that we were sailing to the area where their submarine had sunk.

I had great concerns that they would not turn us back - I shared them with Keys.

"They won't. Certainly not to you, and as I knew, filming and diving into a shipwreck is forbidden, although it is located in the territorial waters of another country. It's complicated, but we're not going to do it. The distance we are interested in is some three hundred meters to the side of the wreckage."

In the morning of the second day, Jacqueline rings on our satellite phone during breakfast.

"You already know?" She asks.

"What do we know?" You hear the concerned voice of Gregor as he gets up from the table and goes out on deck.

He returns five minutes later with a gray face.

"What happened?" Keys asks with fear in her voice.

"During the night, the ship slipped into the depths of the ocean. It is one thousand and eighty meters below the surface. I mean... what's left of it lies," he adds.

It makes things easier for us, I thought badly.

We all knew that there had been no bodies of drowned sailors on the ship for a long time.

"It's just a wreck now," says one of the divers.

He's right - it's just a wreck. But not for Gregor and the others on his crew.

Keys didn't make breakfast or dinner. She only put products on the table in the form of a Swedish buffet and everyone was handling himself. The coffee and tea machine was permanently attached to the table in the wardroom, and the milk was in the fridge. It gave her more time. If she was in a good mood and had it all the time, you could ask her for fried eggs.

I used this privilege most of the time because I liked scrambled eggs and she knew it. The lunches were simple but plentiful so no one went hungry and there were no voices of dissatisfaction among the crew.

On the third day at dawn, we were there. There was no ship or warship in the entire region. Empty, only a slight breeze ruffled the surface of the ocean, closing another page of the sea tragedy.

Bill surveyed the land with me and the helmsman in search of traces of a former whaling settlement. We knew that there must be a bottom conducive to an anchorage, because once the whaling ships stood there for months.

The rose-gold sun showed its face from behind the horizon.

"The weather will be good," said Bill. Keys brought us coffee to the bridge.

"Have you found it yet?" She asked.

"I suppose so," Bill said. He sailed even closer to land.

"Here we will drop anchors and go ashore with our pontoon."

The thud of the anchor chain pounding on the key woke the entire crew asleep.

"Get up, you lazy!" Bill yelled playfully. With Keys I watched from nearby shore. We were alone on the fore deck.

"It sunk here?" She asked.

"No, there, about three or four hundred meters away," I show her with my hand.

The quiet bay where Bill had anchored was to be our base.

"First we go and look for any traces of these stones on the land," I say to Keys. She stands beside me, propped up on my shoulder, and hugs me.

"Are we going to throw wreaths now?" She asks.

"Yes, now, as soon as possible after arriving."

This is the official destination of our trip here. We told everyone around that we were going there to commemorate the victims of the catastrophe. Which, after all, was not far from the truth.

After breakfast, everything was ready. The pontoon was hitting our side and was waiting for us. Keys put wreaths there and fresh flowers, which she kept in the cold room, so that they would not wither. Everyone wanted to throw in their wreaths personally, so we split into two groups.

"Exceptionally, I'll go with the other group, too," Bill tells me. "Then you will stay on the ship."

"He trusts you," notes Keys.

In the first group, Gregor, a reporter, cameraman and Mona, the only female diver, who knew Keys well, is with us.

The sad but necessary activity took us half an hour. Then the second, larger group and we were ready to go to the former whaling settlement.

I loaded the pontoon with everything I thought I needed for this search trip. I didn't know what we were going to get there, but I took two flashlights, a warning device, a coil of thin but strong rope, binoculars, the TV crew had a satellite phone, so only two more radios, a toolbox and... good intentions.

"And what if we meet a polar bear?" Keys says suddenly.

I was stunned.

"Could these bears be here?"

"They can."

"Then why are you talking about it now? I would take a machine gun," I'm kidding her.

But with that in mind, I say to Bill:

"Give me a rocket launcher and two smoke candles. Maybe Keys is right.

We were six people. The helmsman of the Medusa was swimming along the shore a short distance before Keys saw through her binoculars a huge mass of white whale bones.

"There, there!" He calls, over the faint rattle of the engine.

We landed efficiently at what had once been a wooden quay, now only single oak piles were sticking out, showing their jagged stumps out of the water. Nothing left of the settlement but these white bones, which probably and in a hundred years will be stuck here as remorse for the people who murdered these mammals.

Nearby, some remnants of old metal were scattered on the ground. We pass them and go a little higher.

"What do you want to find here?" Roxana asks. "What are we filming?" She adds.

"We are looking for stones," Keys leans. Startled, she looked at me.

"Now you can tell them about these stones, but nothing else," I say to her in an undertone.

"Well, shoot and listen," she says like a movie star, making fun of them.

But then she carefully explains:

"We want to find two rows of stones placed by a human hand, about one hundred and fifty meters long and about thirty meters wide. They are located inland from the shore. You have the ability to get closer, so look for it," she asks the cameraman.

We walked along the shore, looking at our feet. After fifteen minutes the cameraman shouts:

"I think I have it!" He shows us with his hand a very hilly terrain at a considerable distance from us. We walk quickly towards the shore, from where we can see the stone road climbing upwards.

We are standing in the middle of these two rows of stones. But they are no longer symmetrically arranged, sometimes you cannot see them at all, disappear somewhere overgrown or sprinkled with earth.

"It's natural," I say to Keys, so many years have passed since they were put together.

"What now?" Everyone asks me. They know that I play first fiddle here and that the trip is my work.

"Hole. Look for a hole in the ground. It can be small or masked. It's definitely here. Keys, line them all up and scour the area slowly."

We set off from the water side, each a few meters apart. I wasn't sure what I was saying, but logic was telling me that it had to be this way or that it had been so. Three hours of searching and nothing. No trace, no clue. And yet here there are no buildings, trees, bushes, barren land, speckled with stones, boulders, and here and there are growing lichens and clumps of some grass.

On the left, a hundred meters from where we searched the area, there were a dozen large blocks of rock. There were still quite a few of them and that's where Keys and Mona headed their steps.

"We have to aside," she told me, and they left.

After a few minutes, we all hear screams. They both stand and wave at us.

"Quick, quick!" Keys shouts. Standing with warm pants lowered to the knee. Fortunately, she has a long jacket that covers her hips.

Out of the corner of my eye, I notice that the cameraman doesn't run like us, but films everything.

One by one we run to the girls.

"There, look over there!" She says, showing the boulder lying next to her.

You can't see anything until we got quite close, that a black cavity appeared from the base of the boulder.

Small, not visible, you can walk by and not notice anything. If she hadn't crouched here, we wouldn't have been found it - I think to myself.

Meanwhile, Gregor looks at the boulders.

"Richard! Come see," he shows me the boulder in front of himself.

I come closer, followed by the operator. I can see that the side of the boulder is of a different color than the rest.

"What does that say?" I ask Gregor.

"It was done by a man's hand."

"Yeah, of course. Keys, what do you think about it?"

"They blew up boulders, but how? Water and frost or dynamite?"

"Both," says Gregor.

It is impossible to enter it without knocking down the boulder that covered it. The gap you can see is thirty centimeters wide by one meter, one and a half long. It's not enough to enter, but enough to let a flashlight.

I tie my flashlight, light it, and drop it on the rope.

Darkness, you can't see anything but bright light.

Keys sticks her face to the floor and tells us:

"You can't see anything, it must be deep and wide here. The light illuminates nothing.

The flashlight lands lower and lower, already about twenty meters deep, and only now do I sense that it is catching on something. Rolling down, it illuminates the rocks for a moment. Then it descends freely again, but the light is no longer visible, only a faint glow, as if it is blocked on one side.

"Why don't we drop a torch there?" proposes the steersman.

"God forbid, not this!" I firmly object.

I take out my flashlight.

"We're going back," I'm saying enough for today. They looked surprised.

"You don't want to get there?" Mona asks.

"I want to, but not from here," I answer.

We came back at noon. The weather is still nice. We make a sit-in in the mess room, eat dinner and discuss the situation.

"You will go down to the water today to read the conditions and get used to the flow," Bill sets goals.

"Diving into an underwater grotto tomorrow morning," reveals the purpose of our expedition to them. "It can be difficult, strong current and almost vertical wall, you will have to be very careful. Richard was already there, he did not enter the cave because he was without safety and proper equipment. He will tell you about all the dangers."

The TV crew sat with their mouths open and didn't know whether to film or call the boss with these revelations.

"We don't have an underwater camera," the operator noted in a tearful voice, squirming in his chair and tapping a fingernail at his nose.

"We have, we have, don't worry. There will be photos." Keys grimaced, looking at him.

I told everyone what my discovery of the rock breach looked like.

"If it's a grotto," I say to them, because so far I do not know anything for sure. However, these and other clues, including the "poppy field", say that it may be an underwater cave.

Gregor explained to them the meaning of the "poppy field" and the purpose it probably served.

"What if you are wrong and these are the mines?" One of the divers asked.

"They are not mines, but pots and most likely they are made of glass," he sticks to his, or rather Big Ear, arrangements.

I share his opinion on this because in some parts of the "poppy field" some "poppies" are missing, and many of them are chipped like broken bottles.

Now Bill has taken the initiative. He assigned tasks to be performed by individuals, set the order of descent into the water and the safeguards to be used.

"Now two hours of relax, go to the cabins," he ordered.

In a moment you can hear the roar of the engine, the rattle of the lifting anchor and the "Medusa" moves towards the rock chasm. He will drop the anchor close to the shore, in front of the entrance to the cave we discovered on land. From there we will go down to the water.

"I'm very nervous," says Keys, sitting next to me. "Is it very dangerous?" She asks.

"If there was no water current, for us it would be a school trip to the mountains, and this is the climbing of members of the mountain lovers club," I say vividly.

"Anchor down, raft ready, two hours gone," Bill reminds us.

I am the first to go down with Leon, one of the divers, the other two cover us from the deck. Next to the finished pontoon with the helmsman and the third scuba diver inside and a lit engine, puffing calmly at low revs, waits glued to the side of the ship.

Bill used double safety.

I feel a thrill intensified by the hope of discovering the underwater entrance to the cave.

We agreed that we would not penetrate what we found there, but only find out if it was a cave or just a hole in the rock.

"Half an hour maximum," Bill reminds us as he personally checks our equipment once again. Pulls the safety line latch and commands:

"Into the water," simultaneously pressing the stopwatch button.

We are dressed in modern thermal suits with two cylinders on the back. With the camera on my forehead, I slowly descend the ladder, staring at Keys's uncertain expression.

I don't dive right away, just wait for Leon, the second diver.

When he appeared beside me, we slowly plunge deeper and deeper, headlong down the cliff. When we come out from behind a rock overhang, we see a majestically undulating "poppy field", and on the side we are looming in the blue depths, a black stain in the rocky cliff, cut off from the surrounding water. I guess the overhang and the steep ridge of the rocky cliff made it impossible to see from the surface.

Now I increased the descent rate. After a few moments, jerked by the current, we got close enough to the breach that we could easily see the entrance, several dozen meters wide, looked like a wedge from the base upwards, with a sharp beak ending upwards like a signpost for the lost.

The base of the wedge - sixty meters - was estimated by eye. The height of the tear - about forty. We'll measure it carefully later, I decide.

Leon is waving his hand at me, so I follow him right in the middle of this huge gap in the rock. He is right: why fight the flow here? It must be quiet inside there, because the current does not get there.

We're already inside, three or four meters deep. We turn backwards and see the current slide down the slope and disappears below, bouncing off the opposite side of the tear, creating water swirls full of circular, small and larger funnels in the entrance. By shining the flashlight, we can barely see the sides of the cave. I look at my watch - fifteen minutes. We look inward all the time, but our light doesn't reach anything. The dark and mysterious interior tries to discourage us from further wandering. Here and there, only small shoals of fish pass quickly, flashing colorful colors. A small group of orange-black flat fish, perhaps scattered by our beams of light, spins wheels in the light of flashlights, unable to decide which way to run.

We are still swimming for a dozen or so meters deeper. It's getting darker. We stay so close to each other that we rub our shoulders. I nudge him, "there" - point to my right side. He understood and follows me sideways. After a while we reach the side wall.

"We're not going any further," I wave him my hand. It is too dangerous, we can get confused and there will be trouble. Behind us, a bright spot appears behind us, showing us a way out of this huge gap.

"We're going back," I show him my thumb pointing up.

Leon took the initiative and went first, showing me to follow him. OK, why not? I know he is a true professional and I am just a vocational "amateur". As I follow it, I can see it well against the bright glow of the entrance in the darkness. We swim up, chasing our air bubbles that run away from us and scare off some strange creatures. Almost all transparent, having found themselves in a beam of bright light, they do not seem to know that they are being illuminated. Only the touch of the air bubbles scares them away and they quickly hide in the rock chasms.

We quickly cover these several dozen meters, hitting the place where both side walls of the cave join. There is no siphon here, the entire space is flooded with water. But I know it has to be somewhere.

We swim outside, sticking quite close to the rock face, and rush up quickly towards the visible surface. After a while we are about a hundred meters from the ship. Seeing our orange heads on the surface, the helmsman quickly approaches us in a pontoon.

Good method - think about its way to the surface. Strength is saved by not struggling stream.

We calmly return to the ship. Smiling Keys is looking at me, leaning against the rail. Everybody are waiting with curiosity for what we will tell them.

We took off our gear and suits.

"Speak," I say to Leon.

The camera is shooting all the time and Roxana holds the microphone for him.

"This is a grotto. It has a large wedge-shaped entrance with a base at the bottom. Huge, we swam for about twenty meters. It goes on, it is not known how far, because our light did not reach the end. You have to prepare headlights, direction lines, buoys and bottom signals, life-saving appliances, and then keep on going. It's just that and that much," he ends satisfied.

"Okay, second team: get the equipment ready. The three of you go down. You with Richard: dinghy belay," Bill commands. "Half an hour's break," he adds to the sweetness, but only to us, because the rest is bustling, putting all the equipment into the raft.

Keys throws a flashcard from our amateur underwater camera into her laptop and everyone can see the progress of our escapade.

We use this short break to drink a little coffee, watching the same shots from our camera over and over again, paying special attention to the "poppy field".

Both satellite phones keep warm with fresh news.

Gregor calls Jacqueline and the reporter calls the boss. Everyone who is excited expects some sensation, not knowing what will happen next.

"Richard, how did you know about the cave? What could be there?" the interview lady asks, glancing sideways at the laptop screen.

"I got there because of a mine from the time of

World War II," I say to the camera, "and what is there, I do not know, but I can guess. It's not that hard to guess what this underwater cave is hiding."

"Gosh, what is this?!" She calls at the sight of the "poppy field", interrupting our mini interview.

"A hint on how to get to the cave," Bill describes its destiny succinctly.

I think he's right. When a black spot in the rock appears on the screen, we already know that it is someone's hidden secret.

But whose and from when?

The second team of divers quickly expedited with the preparation of the site for tomorrow's trip. They stretched the safety lines, attaching them to the rock wall. With a few headlights they pulled up a cable, the end of which dangled from a small buoy next to our ship.

They placed three life-saving appliances in the entrance - a supply of oxygen for unexpected situations.

The bottom signals were suspended from a larger buoy, marking the direction of the entrance to the cave.

"Is it a grotto or a cave, actually?" Keys asks.

"You know what, I don't know well. I think a bit of both," I settle her doubts.

We talked for a long time in the wardroom about the expedition that awaited us tomorrow, competing in inventing different versions of tomorrow's events. Eventually Bill chased us to our cabins.

In the morning the motorman onboard ship, one of the sailors, Gregor and Keys landed in a dinghy on the shore in front of the boulders, where the entrance to the cave was. The motorman loaded a small combustion nozzle that powered a small, waterproof reflector with a power of several hundred watts.

It was not without a problem that they let it go deeper into the gap until almost the entire power cable was unrolled.

"There's something in there!" Keys called over the radio.

"What you see? Speak," I'm annoyed by her silence.

She lies on the ground like a dead frog, half her head pressed into the crack and finally says:

"Nothing concrete, at least I can't make out what it is, but it must be a structure. It looks like a huge metal container."

"See the water?" I ask.

"No, but something glistens down there on the side, the rest is covered by hanging rock."

"Okay, don't turn off the headlight yet. Once the team is inside the grotto, they will see its light."

"We're waiting for your signal," Keys irritates as she watches both men try to widen the breach by pounding the crack with crowbars. They have already managed to chip off a little bit and widen the gap.

Meanwhile, Ryszard and Leon are already inside the grotto and they are stretching the safety line, attaching it every ten meters to the rocky side of the grotto. On each third hook, they place one floor signal, which now flashes regularly with very intense white light.

"I think we are already at the edge of the shore," thinks Ryszard. You have to try to emerge.

He slowly flows up, releasing the safety line, feeling with his hands a thickening made on it every five meters. It's already twenty meters - there should be a rock vault. But instead of the ceiling, he felt he was in an air chamber. It was two meters to the top wall. He shone his flashlight around - "this is a small chamber!" he rejoiced.

So there has to be an air supply somewhere.

He tugged the rope three times, and after a moment Leon's head appeared.

"It's OK," he shows him the thumb of his right hand. They float on the surface, illuminating the road with flashlights. Suddenly, the side wall shoots up a steep breach to plunge into the water in a few meters. There must be a corridor up there with an air supply.

They dive beneath this rock fracture and after a while they rise to the surface again. The sight they saw took their breath away and made them dizzy.

They were in a rocky underwater cave, but huge and high. Something like that they did not expect to see. It was at least fifty meters to the upper vault. The grotto hall, sixty meters wide, vanished with a slight curve to the right. From behind that arch they could see a bright glow of artificial light, slightly yellowish. "This is our spotlight!" He thought happily.

Leon prodded him with his hand. "Look!" his hand seemed to speak, showing him the nearby rock walkway.

It's a man's work. They stepped onto this carved pavement without any problems.

Leon carefully removed his mask and took out his mouthpiece.

A little breath - the air is normal, not even stale. He felt a slight breeze on his face. There is a draft - that's good, there must be at least two chimneys where the air is exchanged.

Ryszard removed his mask and flippers without hesitation.

A narrow path carved in the rock led to an invisible bend.

"What's going on there?" He asked Leon. His voice echoed among the rock walls for a long time.

"I have no idea..."

They glow on the opposite side of the water. There is nothing there but a brown rock wall that climbs vertically.

Ryszard suddenly noticed a lamp on the wall above his head, or rather its remains. An industrial, oblong wall lamp, of which only a glass shade has survived, and its wire frame is only a rusty mark on the glass.

"Where did we end up?" He heard a soft question with a hint of fear in his voice. "Afraid or what?" He was surprised.

"To a secret base."

"What base, whose base?" Leon's surprised voice asked for an explanation.

"We'll see in a moment," he replied. Another ten meters and everything will be known. The light of their headlamp lowered by the motorman was already very clear, though it must be relatively far away from them.

They emerged from the bend and onto a plain, now widened sidewalk. What they saw was so unexpected and it is shocking that they both stopped unknowingly.

They heard some misshapen noises, echoes magnified by the many reflections off the rock breaks.

"That voice, where did that voice come from?!" Leon exclaimed in fear.

"Don't be nervous, our people shout from above."

Ryszard stood and did not move. He was so surprised by what he saw that he automatically held his breath. The camera on his forehead registered everything he saw, and the dangling searchlight in the distance enhanced the amazing sight in front of them.

Meanwhile, Keys - feverish - argued over Bill's radio:

"I heard, surely heard a voice down there!"

"If you are right, our people must have reached the dry part of the cave."

"I'm not wrong!"

"Then let them know you heard them."

"How?" She asked.

"See the spotlight?"

"No, but I can see its light."

"Take a radio from the sailor and lower it next to the searchlight. If they're there, they'll get in touch soon."

"Come on, give me your phone quickly!" Keys yells to the sailor.

She wraps it in a clean rag beside the motor generator and, tied it to the cord, slowly and carefully lowers it downward.

All this has been recorded by the TV crew for less than half an hour, when, at the reporter's urgent request, the helmsman brought them here by pontoon.

The hard-working crew members of Medusa widened already so crevice that now a grown man can enter.

"There are traces of a metal ladder there," notes the operator who stuck the camera in the hole, turned on the camera light and is recording.

"Good, it means you can enter there from us. Once you could see the entrance inside."

Ryszard and Leon walked a dozen or so meters along the sidewalk, which was steeply descending, leading to the even, rocky ground.

They both stood on command, silent. In the distance, illuminated by the bright light of their searchlight from above, two submarines were visible. They had no doubts - their distinctive cigar-shaped hulls and the fighting conning tower that grew out of them kept them right.

"U-boats..." Ryszard said.

"Boooats, Boats," rock echo replied.

There were several metal, completely rusty cabinets, appliances and something like pumps or motors against the wall. Then small warehouses or other metal, heavily rusty objects. A little further, off the beaten track, glued to the rock wall opposite the metal footbridge running from the submarine, you could see three large, semicircular, tall, like today's containers, tin structures with open doors and funny round windows.

"This must be their quarters," Leon said, pointing at them.

Ryszard was afraid of what he would see in a moment. He realized that if there were two ships here, so must also be their crew.

Unless everyone has evacuated, he thought quickly. But then a thought struck him: maybe they were cut off from the exit and are still stuck here? But where?

He decided to share this thought with Leon.

"What do you think their crew is here?" He pointed at the ships. They both stood side by side, quite high above the rock level.

"U-478 and U-562," he read the heavy brown writing on their conning towers.

They came even closer.

A searchlight dangled over one of the ships, and a rag bundle swayed beside him.

"What is this?" He asked, pointing to a white rag.

"They sent something down from above."

"Shit, too high. I will not take it. I will come on board," he announced.

He stepped carefully onto the gangplank. It turned out to be solid and rust-free, although after so many years of aluminum, which it was made of was already heavily oxidized in some places.

Then he carefully treaded the ship's deck. But here too, after sixty years, there were no holes in the metal skin.

"They built these ships of solid steel," he said to Leon below.

He stood under a rag that he missed from a meter high to reach it. He started looking for something that would allow him to pull it down. He was about to come back when, after a second, as if guessing his thoughts, the rag lowered himself

Ryszard grabbed his hand. He tugged the line twice, the answer was the same, and then they heard a loud call.

"Ours are screaming from above. We're right below them," added Leon.

"Do you hear me?" Ryszard called into the radio.

"Yes, clearly and loudly," Keys replied.

"We're underneath you, lower the spotlight another five meters down. We are OK. There's a huge chamber here."

"What's in it? Speak, Ryszard!" Keys asked, consumed with curiosity.

"When we come back, we'll tell you," he decided to remain silent.

It's too much of a responsibility for him. What to do next?

"We have to check on the crew," Leon forestalled his question.

They went first to large metal objects. The rock echo answered with a loud screech as they yanked on what had once been a door.

They entered carefully. A fairly large room lit up with the dim light of their spotlight shining through four round windows.

"These are living quarters," Ryszard said, looking around anxiously. The raw metal walls must have been whitewashed in the past. Simple soldier's equipment and simple equipment clearly indicated that the comfort was not taken care of.

He already knew what he would see next. A thought flashed to him, why the Almond Apparition had brought him here.

"THEY are lying there unburied," he said.

"Who?"

"The crew of the warships."

They entered the second room. It was getting darker here, the two heavily soiled windows let little light through. Quivering streaks of strong light from their flashlights caught individual human remains in turn.

Some were lying on bunks, others were sitting on chairs with their heads on tables. A few were on the floor, neatly stacked side by side. Few of them remained - shreds of uniforms tearing out white bones. Some leather belts shoes and insulated jackets that did better.

On an elongated table against the wall were two large metal boxes with the words "ACHTUNG" written on them.

What happened here? The terrifying thought swept over him.

"How did THEY die?" Leon asked.

"I guess violently," he blurted out. "Several people at the table do not die of natural causes," he added.

"You're right, Ryszard."

"We're leaving... I'm feeling faint," he said a moment later, as Ryszard was busy looking at the yellowed sheets of paper on the table.

He turned to him at the words. He directed the beam of light at Leon. He saw that his face was very pale and they left quickly.

"Where are the rest?" Leon asked.

"Probably in the third room or in the middle

Of the ship, but we're not going in there today. It could be dangerous."

They hurried out, shining at their feet so as not to step on the human bones lying everywhere.

They looked up at the overhang illuminated by the searchlight. No - it's impossible to get out this way, at least not now.

"Keys! Can you hear me?"

"Yes, Ryszard. All right?"

"Yes, but we're coming back. We'll be on the surface in about fifteen minutes. Wait for us there."

"Okay, I'll pass it on to Bill."

Ryszard took a few more photos and they dived in the water. The road to the bend of rock was dark and strange.

However, they were swimming calmly next to each other, shining torches up the side wall where they came from. When they found round the bend, they immediately saw flashing lights emergency beacons.

He felt an elbow nudge.

"Faster?" I guess that was the point because he had to flap his fins hard to catch up with Leon. They reached the surface without any problems, next to their position buoy. Colleagues in turn pulled them into the pontoon.

"What is there? Say what you discovered?"

"On the ship, quick!" His pale companion cried. Ryszard was silent.

"What is there?" the steersman with a motorman asked every now and then.

"We will say later, we will not tell it twice," unmoved Ryszard did not let himself be convinced.

He also didn't say a word on the ship until they were all gathered together in the wardroom.

"Listen... What we discovered there is definitely a sensation, but on the other hand, I had a reflection that it should be approached with total seriousness and consider what we will do with it next."

"Don't tire us anymore, tell us what's in there?" Gregor couldn't bear it.

"Pirate's treasure!" The motorman joked.

"For some it will be a treasure, for others it will be a relief to the soul."

"Tell what's in there!" Bill urged.

"Submarines, two U-boats and crew," Leon replied for him.

When he finished his story and spoke in full detail, there was a long silence in the wardroom. Everyone digested what they heard.

The reporter grabbed the phone.

"Leave it, don't call yet. We have to decide together what to do next."

"If you call now, helicopters will be here in three or four hours and your report will be gone."

It convinced her. She put the phone on the table.

"Then what, Richard?" She asked.

"I don't know, we have to make a decision together."

"Bill! You are the captain, what do you propose?"

"We need two more days. During this time, we will conduct one or two more technical reconnaissance. We will do what we came here for, which is a report, and then we will take from there those two boxes that Leon talked about," in a calm, balanced voice, he gave them his opinion on the subject with complete seriousness.

"I know German, I'll see what's in there. You may not know, but during the war my father was sailing in these areas and he died because they were torpedoed by a German U-boat. How he broke through protecting US and Canadian warships was never explained. I owe it to him, to all of them who died then. I was five then," he added in the sad voice of the child whose father had been taken.

We all agreed unanimously, raising our hands in open vote. Later, it took us the whole evening to watch the underwater camera shots we shot during this hour-long escapade.

Monday morning made everyone aware that today there is no chance to dive. There was a bad weather, high waves and gusty winds were not conducive to underwater explorations.

Bill picked up the anchor and headed for the nearby Whaling Bay - how had we managed to baptize this tiny patch of relatively still water.

Morning breakfast in the wardroom is one big radio station - everyone wanted to say something. The night was enough for them to reflect on our new situation. The explosion of ideas was mixed with the real and quite ridiculous whims of our crew.

When the initial frenzy had subsided, Bill made quite a reasonable proposition:

"If we cannot get to the Whaler Cave by the underwater side, we will try to enter it from the top," this is what he called the underwater cave we discovered. "We have some sailors here, what encountered many such problems in their sea work."

"What do you mean?" I asked.

"We'll do something like a ladder at the top, use the equipment we have. We have a pilot gangway, a working aluminum ladder, pulleys, a pair of boatswain benches, a lot of ropes and the right skills to use it all."

"Great idea!" Gregor supported him.

"Sure, if we are to waste here, we do not know how much time and wait for the weather to improve, it is better if we try to enter there from the top."

I was sitting quietly. Let them talk. But they didn't let me be silent for long.

"What do you think, Richard?" Bill asked me.

"You're absolutely right. It shouldn't be that hard. I'm pretty sure there's a second entrance there."

If we can find them, then maybe we can get there quickly and relatively safely.

"Where did this suppose?" Keys asked.

"For a simple reason. This entrance we discovered would not have been able to bring some of the structural elements down there. For example, the big pumps we saw inside."

"They could have delivered them by submarine."

"They could, but I don't think they have the option. They are too big for their cargo hatch, more like a merchant or warship."

The breakfast is eaten up, the coffee is drunk, so we all start working on the tasks Bill gave us. The pontoon turned twice between the settlement and our boat.

The third time, it carried all but one seaman, motorman and Bill. The weather was too unstable and the captain didn't want to leave his Medusa unattended.

It took us a long time to bring it all to the cave entrance that was visible next to the boulder.

When we attached the aluminum gangway to the boulder next to it, I climbed down on it.

The darkness scattered by the ship's searchlight showed Ryszard the raw face of the rocky breaches in this solid block, probably torn apart by some very ancient movement of tectonic plates running somewhere in the depths of the earth.

The descent turned out to be more accessible, but invisible from above. Two meters to the side where their aluminum ladder ended, a wide, rock-cut staircase ran. They led a slight serpentine up.

The entrance is probably there, well disguised.

We'll deal with it later, Richard thought.

The other part of the stairs missed the overhang and with a gentle slope it descended to the very ground, finishing its course on the other side of the ships - right at their prow.

Who and when forged these stairs? Reflection came to him. The color of the rock stone clearly stood out from the color of the other rocks. In his mind's eye he saw emaciated prisoners of war or some other unfortunates that the Nazis had sent to do these hard work. Because they probably didn't do it themselves - what happened then to them was easy to guess.

They certainly didn't take them back to where they had taken them.

His task was to move the ladder so that its last rung would hang directly above the winding down stairs. And then fix it rigidly so that it does not sway under people coming down from it. It took him some time to drive two large hooks into the rock crevices, to which he tied the other end of the ladder.

"Now you can go down," he said over the radio.

"One by one," he added. All but two of the crew of the Medusa, whom the captain had ordered to stay above, had descended.

"For safety reasons, not everyone can go down there right away," he ordered. "You'll come down in the second round," he added for sweetness.

Now they had two large lamps, dismantled for that time from the ship's wings, effectively illuminating the entire chamber. It is also for the sake of safety and to the satisfaction of the team filming our entire escapade.

Nobody left, they just waited quietly in the group until everyone was downstairs.

Gregor took the initiative. As a submarine, he was well versed in all aspects of submarines, even if they were German U-boats.

"Keys, two divers and a TV crew doing research around the ships. Film everything and comment on it on an ongoing basis, it will be a documentary record," he assigned them a task.

They stood and dutifully nodded, overwhelmed by what they had seen, and anxiously thinking about what they had not yet seen.

"Me, Richard and Leon and the helmsman are going to the U-boats. We will film everything with our amateur camera. Communication via radios, check if they work," he said at the end.

"Hello! How do you hear me?" Keys rumbled an echo in the rock chamber.

"Okay, not so loud!" Gregor confirmed. With flashlights and a long line with them, they headed for deck of the first one. It was the U-478.

The hull and the entire plating of the U-boat were not in such a bad condition that it was impossible to move around on it. They walked across the deck, the open cargo hatch inviting them inside.

Ryszard felt uncomfortable, before, but on another ship, he also penetrated its interior in this way and found the Almond Apparition, now he knew that he would also find dead people from this ship's crew. That's why he stayed close to Gregor.

"First visit in so many years," he said to Gregor.

"But no one is expecting us on that side," he replied, walking down the metal rungs to the first deck.

"Certainly no one of the crew, but there are a lot of documents that will be a tasty morsel for historians," he kept the conversation going, knowing that it encouraged everyone.

But the crew had waited sixty years for them. They were everywhere. They lay in bunks one above the other, in a small wardroom and in command positions. Two of them, in the remnants of white coats, lay in a orlop on the deck.

"Probably Cook and his helper," said Leon. "They died where they stood... But why?" He asked himself and the others this question.

The specific climate of the rock grotto made them shine now with black eye sockets made of white skulls, which, with the flashlights moving in our trembling hands, intensified the already terrifying sight. The horror of the moment, the stale air inside the ship, and the feeling that these skeletons were about to get up to say hello inspired the urge to flee immediately from this place to the open space. It is the second time in such a short time that he is in a submarine with a flashlight in his hand and the dead inside. It's too much even for him.

"I'm going out," he thought. "I'm just gonna get something I came in here for." "Gregor, where's the ship's log?" He asked. "That's the only thing I want to take away from here."

"Usually there is a special place in the command post. Or in the captain's cabin."

"Lead on," he asked.

The captain's cabin was not far away, a few meters behind the fighting conning tower, it greeted us with an open door. A tiny cubicle with a single berth and a folding sink with a cupboard overhanging it, a small table next to it, with a few loose sheets and an open logbook.

*May 8, 1945*

A few lines in fine, even writing appeared on its open side. Record most likely by the captain's hand, whose remains fell to the floor after a possibly suicide shot in head. The gun was still lying beside the skeleton's right hand. He shuddered at the thought that came over him: to turn that skull away and see if he has a hole in his head. He didn't have to do it, however, because it was Gregor who stood so unhappily that he stumbled and staggered, took two uncontrolled steps, rubbing his skull with his left foot. It rolled into a corner with a soft scuffle.

A flashlight beam followed her. There was a hole in the right temple.

"Oh shit, I'm sorry," said Gregor. Is he apologizing to me or the captain? "It's all sad," he says to him though. "However, fate is sometimes just. Only in this case?" I ask him a question.

"What are you talking about?" Leon asked.

"About the stairs."

"I don't understand," he just said, rummaging through the open safe. What was he looking for there? Maybe old ciphers or other documents? Regardless, Ryszard already had what he came here for.

"We're leaving," he just said.

Without a word, they followed him to the exit.

As they left and stood on deck, Keys waved at them and, sobbing softly, said:

"I won't go in there a second time," the echo strengthens her voice.

"You don't have to, wait for me here," he also answered her in a low voice, which still, enhanced by the acoustics of the chamber sounded with an unnatural timbre.

They rested a bit and moved on to the second submarine: U-562.

Here, however, they found only the remains of the crew in the wardroom and in bunks. Everyone else seemed to have left the ship in a hurry. There were rotten clothes, documents, scattered personal belongings everywhere.  There was nothing in the command post or in the captain's cabin. The safe and desk were empty.

"They took it all outside," said Gregor.

"Yes, they were probably the crew of the second ship and not all of them slept on the ship, most of them slept and lived in these steel quarters. It's always a substitute for home. Perhaps, after all, they were waiting for the other ship, and when it arrived, this tragic end came?"

"What are you talking about again?"

"That they all died a sudden and unnatural death here."

"Yes, you are probably right. At least Cook and the captain and the rest of the crew died where they stood," he said.

He went outside. Gregor and the rest of them still looked into various rooms of the ship, and Ryszard with Keys sat on some concrete box.

"Come on, let's go back," Keys asked.

"I can't, I have something else to do."

"What?" Her voice is surprised. She looks at him with teary eyes. He sees that she has experienced a shock. Not only she - everyone was quiet, moody, even the TV crew no longer filmed or asked any questions.

"Are we waiting for the rest?" She asked.

"Yes, we'll all leave together," he confirmed.

"Bill, this is Ryszard," he calls over the radio. The motorman upstairs intercedes this conversation because there is no direct connection with Bill.

"We need diving equipment - two sets. Send us this waterproof reflector as soon as possible. I will want to illuminate the bottom of the chamber."

"Okay, I'm sending it now," he replies, without even asking what this is needed for.

In the meantime, the rest left the second U-boot.

"I think we've seen everything, the rest is not ours," says Gregor. "It's time to go back."

"Not everything yet," says Ryszard. "I have to go down here. It won't take long. Wait a little longer."

"Will you protect me?" he asks Leon.

"Okay, no problem."

Two cameras, suits and a reflector flashing with light are already coming down.

They both get dressed quickly.

"Give me the camera," Keys pleads, hooking it to his forehead with Velcro.

He picks up the reflector and slowly sinks down the stern of the U-boats to the very bottom. It is not deep here - from the surface of the water it is about fifteen or twenty meters.

It flows above the very bottom along the rocky cliff, illuminating it with a searchlight. He had already swam the entire distance, to the break of the rock - and nothing. He feels Leon sensitively loosen his safety line.

"Am I wrong in my assumptions?" He wonders.

Now on the other side of the chamber, you need to check the bottom here. It slowly moves along the second rock wall of the chamber, but there is nothing but silt. He flows to the corner of the chamber, where the stone steps end above the water, and in the light of the spotlight he sees a skull, a human skull. Then the bones - more and more human skeletons lay at the bottom.

He rises to the surface with a heavy heart and soul on his shoulder. He sits down heavily on the beam, with Keys' help he takes off his mask and suit and remains silent.

Finally Gregor can't stand it and asks:

"And what?"

"I found them," he says. "They're over there in the corner," he shows which corner it is.

"Who, who?" the reporter asks.

"Prisoners killed by the Germans! There are many, many of them. We're leaving," he croaks through his throat, still clenched with sensation. "I'm sick of this place."

Keys hugs him lovingly.

"Your mission is over, it will be okay," she comforts him.

All the moody ones, overwhelmed by what they had seen and what they had heard from him - returned to the ship.

They moved quickly to the booths. It was still an hour until dinner, but they didn't stay there too long, and after a while they all met again in the wardroom. They sat around a rectangular table, facing the entrance was a double sofa. This is the place for the captain and watch officer.

The rest on both sides were occupied in the order of coming, because there was not much free space for a free passage after you sat down at the table. I sat on the corner and waited for Keys. When she sat down with us for a moment, it was obvious that she had to let go of her accumulated doubts about the views from the grotto.

"What happened to them?" She asked.

"Maybe they didn't have fuel to get out of there, or the ice in the grotto hadn't been released yet and they died of hunger and cold," the steersman reveals his thoughts, stirring the soup in his plate with a spoon.

"It's not impossible that there was icing there in May. I think that the water in the grotto did not freeze even in winter," Leon interrupted him.

"Then what happened there?" he continues to ask Keys.

"We'll probably find out sometime," Bill interrupted, pouring soup into his plate.

"Enjoy your meal, ladies and gentlemen. Now dinner and enjoyable topics."

They ate lunch, drank coffee, and took to the dinghy and set off for land.

Now I stayed with the rest of the ship, and Bill and two sailors, a steersman and one diver went to collect all the equipment for us.

"Bill, will you go down to the cave?" I asked.

"No, I don't want to watch this. The photos you took are enough for me. But the guys will come down, I can't stop them."

"Sure, let them see it for themselves - it's better than any history lesson."

They came back tired and so depressed.

That evening, we raised the anchors and headed back to Naomi.

During the dinner, we agreed that we would not wait for what our authorities would do, and that the recorded material would be enough to compose a sensational report from our trip.

"Richard, how did you know about these prisoners?" Roxana asks me, ending my contract interview.

"Stairs. Stone stairs carved into the rock. For this history lessons," I answer.

"Explain it to us, because I have no associations."

"You can't have them because Canada wasn't under German occupation, and you are too young and too little read," I thought, but I said aloud:

"From the history lessons about the times of the Second World War and the Nazi occupation, I knew that the Germans used prisoners of war to build various military fortifications, shelters and more, and then liquidated them on the spot so that the secret of these places would remain a secret. Stone stairs carved in the rock could not have been the work of submarine sailors... "Lords of the World" did not bother with such works, having countless people from the nations they conquered. I just don't know who those unfortunates were and how they got there, but historians will find out and then we'll find out."

The discussion about the German crew did not last long.

"What happened to them?", "Why and how did they die?" these were the most frequently asked questions. After heated discussions, we agreed to accept two variants of events:

First - they were put to sleep by someone from the crew and then killed. And the captain who survived was left alone and did suicide.

The second - they were poisoned by the captain who later committed suicide.

However, the real cause of their strange deaths will only be revealed by the results of the research, which will certainly be done, and then it will be known how they died.

On the way back, we were busy watching the footage we had shot and answering numerous phone calls from various important people. We revealed what we discovered, without revealing the place where the secret base was located.

On the quay in the port, crowds of people, military authorities, reporters and journalists waited for us, and finally the families of the "Medusa" crew who could not crush to us.

My interview was over, and so was my role in this whole endeavor. Except for one meeting I couldn't not to go: at the request of Naomi City Council, I was made an honorary citizen.

"Now just apply for Canadian citizenship and you will automatically get it," maire of the city advised me.

I did so and after a few days I became a Canadian. As Jacqueline said, it was the Canadian Navy Command that had a hand in it. "They gave their opinion on your application," she explained to me when I was surprised by the pace of obtaining citizenship.

I went to one of the banks and set up an account - this was on the advice of William, who in the contracts with TV included my account number, which was to be influenced by cash from each broadcast of the report from our trip.

The hype around this case lasted a whole week. Diplomatic notes from several countries clashed about the rights to everything that was in this cave.

Somehow, nobody remembered about our rights. It's good that we took care of them ourselves.

I did not agree to any other meetings later, interviews and visits to distinguished Canadian offices and institutions. Splendor and the resulting responsibilities of the other participants of the expedition took it upon themselves. I wanted have a peace and go back home. I have already re-book my ticket to Warsaw.

I'm flying in three days.

There was also the case of two crates with the inscription "Achtung".

On the way back, we opened the smaller one first. I don't know German, but Bill skimmed through all the documents.

"These are codes, ciphers, orders, crew list, spare parts inventory and other such documents. However, there is no log for the second U-boat."

"Perhaps I can find out from them what ships they sunk?" He got feverish at the thought.

In the second, larger, there was a cipher machine. It is packed in a wooden box and sealed. German pedantry... Why didn't they destroy it? - I was wondering. They knew it was over, or maybe they still hoped that Hitler's "secret weapon" would be able to make a difference.

I gave everything to Bill.

"Take it. It is the property of our entire crew, see and if you deem it necessary, then sell it or return it to the museum. Do what you see appropriate.

"Thanks Richard, I'm sure I'll make good use of this."

I deposited the U-487 Logbook at Gregor.

"Take it and store it. When I come back, you will give it to me. I have no chance of taking it to Poland, which is the only thing I would like to keep."

"Easy, I'll put it in your bank vault and send you the number. You can always get it from there yourself."

Keys was crying and she didn't want me to go to Poland.

"I love you, Richard, don't leave me alone! Stay, you can get a job here, or you can still swim on your contracts. You are famous, you have friends, you will have no problems finding a good job here!"

"Keys, I'll be back in a month, I'll be back for sure. But now I have to go home. I have a mother there, friends and many other things, I can't just leave everything like that!"

I was not sure of my feelings, so after saying goodbye to Keys, the family of Lieutenant Mc Langer and the crew of the "Medusa" I returned to the country, where a very round sum of Canadian dollars from the local TV was waiting for me and it was a source from which I drew a long rustling Canadian money.

William, as always, had a nose for lucrative deals. But the biggest surprise for me was Bill.

One day he called me and asked after some initial courtesies:

"Richard, do you give your consent for these boxes to be returned to the museum in Hamburg?"

I thought to myself: why Hamburg? But I replied:

"Sure, Bill. Do what you see appropriate."

"Did you discover anything interesting in these documents?" I asked, keeping in mind some special mysteries.

"Just one thing for me: that U-boat sank the ship my father was in. I also made copies of all documents, if you want, I will send them to your e-mail."

History has come full circle - I just thought, but said:

"No, it's okay, thank you."

"Okay, then I'll just send you a copy of the letter I found in the coffee bean jar. I already translated it."

"OK, send it."

Curious the next day, I opened an email from Bill.

First, I saw documented photographs of the jar and separately a sheet of paper taken from the jar, which was written in fine handwriting:

*My dear Gertrude!*

*This is my last message to you, you may get this letter, but I am also writing it for those who will one day discover our Secret Base. The war is over and I realized we were going to lose it two years ago.*

*The last mission Hitler personally commissioned us was to take a few dignitaries to Argentina. It turned out, however, that they were SS men themselves. I have listed them all below. Only a small group of SS men knew about this base and only they docked on our U-boat.*

*They exchanged almost all of my crew at Formosa - and were illustrated by their merits for Hitler. Now on my ship there are SS men close to Admiral Karl Dönitz, fleeing like rats from the sinking Motherland.*

*I had no idea where we were going - I didn't know this base existed. They can't get to Argentina, they have blood on their hands, and so is on mine. We were waiting for the second U-boat with supplies and the national treasure of Germany. I saw these crates, they took them away and sunk them. I hid the details of this place in my Ship Log, and the key to it is in this letter. However, they will not get there after they boasted that 63 prisoners of war of various nationalities were murdered here. They were building this secret base in the fortieth year. The SS men murdered them in the forty-first year. It was 32 Russians from Królewiec and 21 Poles from Gdańsk, the rest are Norwegians from Alesung - all prisoners from Stutthof. However, they will never take advantage of them. They will stay here forever - me too. I have already put my plan into practice. I gave them the agent that I had received from our command in case we were taken prisoner.*

*"Herr Captain seems to understand that the crew cannot fall into enemy hands"- these are the words of our Admiral. So I obeyed his order.*

*I love you*

*Hans*

Bill's note below:

"I kept the jar for us. Nobody knows about it, so we are preparing a search expedition. The key to it is in the Ship Log, which is in your hands.

But with that, we have to wait until next summer."

Imagine my surprise when two weeks, the bank in Naomi, in which I had an account, sent me an e-mail statement asking if the forty thousand euros transferred to my account by Bill would convert me into Canadian dollars or set up a sub-account in this currency.

I called Bill.

"What's going on, Bill? Where did this money come from?!" I asked.

"Where did they come from? From the museum, I told you. This is your plot, I divided the entire amount from the sale of these documents to the Hamburg museum to all participants of the expedition. It's good that you are calling me and our entire team are inviting you for a few-week trip to the Caribbean - to the local coral reefs. You probably don't know, but we sold the Medusa, we added some money from these shares and we bought a new boat. Beautiful, come and welcome. We're sailing in two months."

"I'll think about it and let you know. Thanks, Bill."

Keys called me every day and she showed up on Skype at night so I thought I knew about everything that happened there - but it was not so.

They wanted to surprise me and they succeeded.

After less than a month, a smiling Keys landed at the Warsaw airport. During her stay in Poland, I rented quite a large apartment in Monciak. I cannot live with her in my little apartment in Karwiny, and my house is still not finished.

# Chapter IX

# Caribbean

***Saturday, November 14***

They circled us. Four large beasts with glass eyes staring at their dinner.

Joined by our arms, we formed a tight circle and we looked anxiously through the masks with pipes sticking out into the sky at the pontoon approaching us. Who will be faster, those hungry sharks attacking with lightning speed or our colleagues on the pontoon too far away for us to wait for them in calm?

"We're shooting," Leon asked, aiming his crossbow at the nearest shark.

"We shoot, but all of us in one," I replied.

Keys holds my hand tightly. She alone does not have a crossbow.

"What should I defend myself with?" She asks, but there is no fear in her voice.

"Here, take it," and I unclip my sailor khanjali from my right drumstick. Razor-sharp and long as a bayonet. "Hit him in the eyes," I lecture her calmly.

One of the instructors points at the shark, which is the first to start making narrower and narrower circles:

"In this one, he will attack soon! Now!" He calls.

The three needle-sharp blades of the crossbow stick into his body, rivulets of blood appeared around him.

The shark rolls around its axis and then I hit into his exposed belly, right into his heart which is hidden under the gills.

Confused by this sudden attack, he snaps out of rhythm and accidentally hits the other shark. That was enough, blood starts to color the water around them. One of the sharks tore a chunk of meat from his back. It rattled next to us.

"Run!" Leon screamed, and the instructor and I started going away from this tangle of slender shark bodies.

They're cannibals, I thought as I pulled Keys back towards the dinghy.

The eternal spectacle of man-eating shark tactics was taking place before us. A quick attack from a short distance, a snap of a wide jaw against the body, a few jerks of the enormous head and also a quick jump back, so that you can easily eat a piece of torn meat.

Meanwhile, the pontoon passed us on the left, getting closer to the other sharks fighting for the remains of their recent companion. Flowing between us and the sharks, they made a circle, throwing orange-yellow powder into the water, directly on the engine bolts. The water instantly changed color, creating a strip of opaque water veil several meters wide. Only now did they start dragging us into the pontoon. Keys and Mona first went to the pontoon, then all the rest of us.

Keys laughed first, then Mona and finally everyone else burst out into nervous laughter.

"What's so funny?!" One of the instructors cried, red on the face, it is not known whether the powder or the sensations.

Perhaps only he was aware of the seriousness of the situation in which we had just found ourselves.

"To base," said the steersman.

The pontoon was quickly approaching the new acquisition of our club of lovers of underwater experiences.

Ours, because Bill and the rest of the crew surprised me by enlisting me as an equal shareholder of their club.

"If it wasn't for you, there would be no 'Shell'," that's what they called their new ship. "Therefore, we all unanimously voted this idea," he informed me, giving a notarized entry in the books.

"Thank you very much, but it was unnecessary... And so I will not have enough time to often go on underwater escapades with you. After all, I am a sailor and I work far from land."

"It's unknown, it isn't known whether it will always be like this," Bill replied, his gaze drifting to Keys who listened carefully to the conversation.

They bought the "Shell" from the Canadian Navy. In age, she was several years younger than their "Medusa", but technologically ahead of her by three decades. This auxiliary ship of the Canadian Navy was much better, its hydrographic service ended three years ago and no one was needed at the end of some forgotten wharf. When it landed in their hands, it underwent a thorough cleaning - some small elements were replaced and their old decompression chamber was installed in a friendly fishing shipyard.

Cabins... Luxury compared to their old boat, there was one bathroom for two cabins. The two entrances to one bathroom were strange. Open your door and close the one in front of you so that no one would come in, and when you left you had to open it again.

How many times pounding the sheet let us know that we forgot to open the bathroom door from the inside.

On the "Shell", each cabin had its own bathroom, a sofa where you could rest, a table and a large berth. A comfortable, spacious mess and a modern kitchen are a real convenience for Cook. Everything sparkled with stainless steel, there was a dishwasher and a modern oven. At the stern, there was a small davit for a pontoon and a lot of space, because this former hydrograph carried buoys, floating beacons and other equipment, so it had to have a lot of space. The "Shell" engine was unbreakable, and the wheelhouse was equipped with all the latest navigation devices. They are ten years old, but on their "Medusa" they were even older, and here there was even sonar. And most importantly, there was "Michałek" - an automatic helm and a collision indicator. Bill was delighted and so were the rest. It took them two weeks to repaint the "Shell" from steel gray to white and the same amount of time to load and adapt the diving equipment. Then we set off on the first expedition.

It was several days ago when we set off for the Caribbean.

Now, however, we quickly said goodbye to our underwater guides - two local Colombians - and settled in the spacious wardroom.

"What the hell was that?" Leon blurted out. "There are no sharks here."

"Where did these beasts come from?" Keys is surprised.

"Do you know what I remember?" Mona says, with one elbow on the table and the other stroking Leon's jet-black hair.

"Oh, it's probably already a couple," I thought as I watched her lightly brush his hair. His eyes narrowed and glowed with a gleam of satisfaction.

"What?"

"As we were yesterday in this restaurant on the old pier by the beach. I was sitting with Keys at a table, and you went to the local instructors to talk about tomorrow's coral Dream Goddess expedition - as local fishermen call this reef. Keys walked over to you, and in a moment a young girl, the mother of little Luisa, who had been following me from this morning, approached me."

Little Luiza did not leave Mona behind. From the moment she saw her, every day she was waiting for us at the pier exit. When Mona appeared on the horizon, she was already standing by her and smiled with the happy smile of a child who knows that there will be some kind of pleasant surprise for him. And so it was, Mona always had something for her. And this is a sweet bar, and this is chocolate or other treats. However, Luisa didn't like Mona for this reason. They both had long blonde hair - while it was normal for Mona, it was not necessary for little Luisa. She was different from the other dark-haired kids, and Luisa's mom was typically Latin.

When Luisa got a little bold, she asked Mona:

"You know my dad?"

Surprised, Mona looked at her, not understanding. And the little girl calmly explained to her:

"My dad has the same hair as you and me. My mom said he went somewhere in a country where everyone has fair hair and I'm still waiting for him."

"No, baby, I don't know your dad, but when I see him, I'll tell him that you are waiting for him."

"Say I love him," Luisa says to her, looking into her eyes, and I think she believes Mona will tell him. Then she takes her hand and they go to the nearest ice cream parlor.

The little blonde's mom is a waitress in the restaurant where we used to go for lunch. Then she must have heard us learn about the possibility of diving in this area.

"Don't go over there," she said, coming up to me. "It's bad terrain. There you can fall asleep," and she quickly walked away, looking from side to side.

"I don't know Spanish very well, so I thought I misunderstood her. It turns out, however, that she wanted to warn us."

"Before what?" Bill asked.

"Maybe the sharks."

"And the local boys? They wouldn't know about it?"

"I don't know, maybe they don't. Or they know, but the temptation to earn a lot closes their mouths," Keys considers several theories at once.

"Okay, what are we doing now? We were supposed to swim among this coral reef, but when there are sharks, you have to raise an anchor and go elsewhere."

"I like it here, and the sharks won't stay in one place all the time. Anyway, they can be anywhere."

"What about 'bad terrain'?"

"I don't know what she meant, I'll talk to her tomorrow," Mona declares. "And now we're going to the beach, there will be a sand party. Who will go with us?"

We all went. The wonderful white sand, blue-turquoise water floods the shore with a wide wave, walking right up to the sunbed on which I rested. Here and there, the shimmering rays of the sun break through the dried palm leaves arranged on four curved bamboo poles attached to a pole stuck in the sand. A shadow covers my little space, making my body blissfully lazy. I lie still, switching my mind off to the sounds of softly dripping music from a nearby bar reaching me. Bar is a bit exaggerated term. Just a larger piece of a shack covered with a roof made of bamboo and palm leaves, some shelves on which the glass bellies of bottles proudly stick their labels out. But the drinks make delicious here. And they don't cheat on alcohol. And since it is almost free - for us, we drink it in amounts that are dangerous to our heads.

The sound of the waves and the rhythms of the southern music slowly put me to sleep...

My thoughts go back to Poland. The time of perestroika is over, and in PRO, the division of our company into two independent companies is just beginning.

Two separate companies - PRO and the SAR Service (Search And Rescue) were created, where is my place? - I wonder.

In addition, Keys flew in. I was very happy about it, but because of that, I did not have time to think about which one I would like to work for.

Like a bolt from heaven, a call came from the Petronafta Company in Gdańsk. They were forming a partnership there with the Americans, and something from Canada leaked about me to them.

They invite me to a job interview.

"Don't go, you'll find a better job at us," Keys tries to convince me.

She still hopes to live with her in Canada. However, I left her in the care of my friend Krzysztof and I went to them.

The visit did not last long. A short conversation with their boss ended with his declaration:

"You have a job. When can you start?" Not much thought, I replied:

"Only in six months. There are a lot of things I have to finish here and there."

"I understand when you will be ready, please report."

So, now I have six months of vacation.

I don't have to worry about the money - the Canadian source is not dry yet.

"Keys!" I am calling from the door of Krzysztof's restaurant, "we are going into Poland, I am free as a bird."

Keys threw herself around my neck, probably misunderstanding my words.

"And then we go back to Canada?" She asks.

"Yes, then we fly to Canada, there is a "Shell" waiting for us, which we will sail to the coral reefs, and then we will take on the hidden treasure," I blurted out inadvertently.

Krzysztof looked at me surprised.

"What treasure?"

"German, actually Hitler's."

"Sit down and tell me right here! What are you hiding?" he is feverish, curious about the topic.

We told him what is what.

"How will it end?" he wonders. "Isn't it better to outsource it to some company with the appropriate equipment?" he asks.

"No, this is our discovery and we will finish our work," Keys proudly assures him.

If my sixth sense had kicked in then, maybe I would have done what Krzysztof advised us to do. But it was silent, and none of us could have foreseen the tragedy that the search for these mysterious chests would end.

After two weeks with Keys, we went back to Canada together.

"And how did you like it in my country?"

"A wonderful, beautiful vacation! I didn't know you had such an interesting history, such monuments and these wonderful forests and lakes, beautiful beaches and so many warm, nice people..."

Suddenly I felt splashes of warm water on me. I quickly opened my eyes. It was Keys, she was splashing at me, laughing happily. In the glare of the setting sun, her deeply tanned skin glistened with water droplets sparkling with salt flecks - it was beautiful. Pride poured all over my body.

"I'll show you!" I screamed like a wolf from a Russian cartoon and I ran after her.

Tonight, not everyone returned to the Shell.

Beach, dance floor podium and stage with a roof covered with palm leaves, the orchestra plays all the world's hits live, occasionally weaving domestic Latin rhythms - rumba, salsa and beloved by me and Keys Argentinian tango, which people dance here completely different than in Canada or Europe.

Watching Latinos give their soul to these rhythms, dancing sensually, exuding sex and staged with every movement, we try to keep pace with them.

After dancing to the rhythm of hot southern music and a lots of drinks we fell to the sand. Some of us slept on deckchairs. All the guests of this bar were watched by specially hired "machos" - nothing unpleasant could happen to anyone here - it would be the end of their business. So they guarded us like their Madonna.

In the late afternoon we were finally gathered in the wardroom.

"No diving today," Bill tells us. "You cannot enter the water with such drunks. They would have deposited all the fish on the reef."

But we were hungry, no breakfast or dinner.

"Don't think I'm going to cook for you here," Keys stormed on the first day. "It is different in the sea, I do not think to do it here."

"Folklore, folks! Have some folklore and local specialties. Lunch is less than a pack of cigarette, so you have no choice." She snapped pots and left the kitchen.

I agreed with her.

Now we went to dinner in unison, and then to explore the nearby town.

We walked the way from the pier, where our "Shell" was moored, then got on a small railway trolley, which was pulled by two scooters attached to its side. Loud growling with their little ones motors, set us in motion. Little boys sat on their saddles, and, holding the handlebars, they watched intently to keep the front wheel from popping off the rails.

"Do they have runs? How do they keep their balance on them?" I wondered until, leaning lower, I noticed that they were bolted to the trolley with some screws. Rims without tires encompassed one rail that led them to their goal of local relics hidden in the jungle.

Dinner - very tasty, only spiced with some local specialty - we ate in a small restaurant tuned to tourists near the ruins of the ancient Inca city - or so our guide said.

The return was very mysterious, because it was lit by burning torches that smoked more than gave light. But it was atmospheric and cheerful, because singing and music performed live by Latin American boys made our time pleasant.

In the morning, a great commotion, we finally anchored over a coral reef. The Goddess of Dreams was waiting for us, shimmering with all the colors of the rainbow and a wealth of fauna and flora. You will not find such colors and various creatures anywhere else - only in the water and on the reef. This is why when someone sees it, they will never forget the sight.

Crazy exciting descent into the water. We go down in pairs. Me with Keys, from the shore side with masks and fins, stick to shallow water. I am only surprised why the pontoon is always close to us. We swim on the surface with our face immersed in water. The pipe sticking upwards supplies us with air. Sometimes taking a deep breath we sink three meters lower than the surface of this fabulously warm and transparent water. Then, gliding over the reef itself, we watch their inhabitants closely. A ray (stingray) moves majestically next to us, its long tail ending with a venomous spike, waving at us to the rhythm of its movements. It's something amazing because it doesn't float in this water, it flies like a bird, moving its broads around - what is it? I wonder. For sure not wings. Probably such triangular fins. They do not have an easy life here, because they are a local delicacy and people catch them so intensely that they are in danger of becoming completely extinct. One more beautiful species may be plotted from the book of life of this planet. Just like this giant turtle, which does not fear us, swims within easy reach of Keys. She touches his colorful shell gently, and he glares at her with a half-closed, large eyelid. Its hilly head, ending in a triangular beaked mouth, opens slowly, as if to tell her, "be careful, baby!"

Keys looks at me, happy that I managed to film it, then comes to the surface to take a breath.

"You got it!" She calls to me.

"Yes, everything is recorded."

We sail to the shore, the wild beach entices us with its white sand and palm trees growing nearby.

We fall to the sand exhausted by our experiences.

"It was worth the long trip," I say to Keys.

"It's worth going where you are," Keys ambiguously commented on my short sentence.

We lie on the sand and look at the long surf breaking onto the beach. Two crewmen on a pontoon are waving at us from a distance.

"They'll come for us. Come on, let's go into the shade," says Keys.

I follow her meekly, where we fall to the sand right behind the first palm trees. Suddenly, out of the corner of my eye, I see a white starfish in the sky. After a while the second.

"They shoot rockets!" I say to Keys.

"We get up, they call us to the ship!" fast picking up our scattered things, we run towards the water. The pontoon at full speed has passed the surf on the reef and is speeding towards us. We jump inside.

"What happened?" Keys asks.

"We don't know, Bill gave the order to immediately collect everyone from the water and return to the Shell," replies our full-time skipper.

We are the last. Everyone on the aft deck is waiting only for us. We pull the pontoon in quickly and "Shell", with an engine roaring, heads towards the port. We're leaving the Dream Goddess far behind. After a while, Bill came down to us, leaving the rudder in the care of the helmsman.

"Speak," he said to Mona, who was the first to return to the Shell deck with Leon supporting her.

"I was swimming along the reef watching the fish, and Leon was at the top of it, about ten meters higher. There she has such a step from the beach. Part of it has a slight curve to the left and turns to the shore. That's when the sandy bottom begins. I was chasing some big fish along this fault line when it suddenly turned towards the reef and hid in its cleft covered with red anemone.

I lay flat on the bottom and peered inside, and there, about two meters from me, I saw a narrow strip of clean water, but enough to swim across it. I nod to Leon, but he doesn't look at me because he's busy teasing the barracuda hidden in a nearby hole and can't see me. It finally comes to me. 'What is?' He waves his hands in yellow gloves in front of me.

'Wait, I'll see what's in there' - I show him a strip of free water. Its firm NO and finger up. Okay, he's right, so we're going to the surface. 'What you want to do?' He asks, taking out the mouthpiece. 'I'll swim in there, there's enough space, I'll see what's in there', 'Okay, two minutes. I'm right behind you.', 'Two OK' - and I dive straight into the hole invisible from here.

I press slowly into a four to six meter long crevice, touched by delicate coral flowers. Its stingers do not make any impression on me, I am wearing a wetsuit, which protects me effectively. I'm just careful about the chin, because it's not covered. I am swimming in a slightly strange position, because with my right side towards the surface, and with my outstretched hand I control the width of the slit. How wide is it? A meter, maybe a little more. Slowly I notice a greater clearance above me and I am already in the middle of a huge, sandy shag. I can't see its end on either the left or the right.

I am swimming along the reef a dozen or so meters and suddenly my eyes see metal cages lying at the bottom, and some boxes inside. They are not big - maybe a meter high and two meters long. There are several of them, they lie at the bottom covered from above by a rocky coral overhang. Next to it, I see with horror hooves, a head with horns, and some animal bones. 'What the hell is this?' - I think. Water burial ground. Curious about where I am, I slowly rise to the surface.

In front of me you can see the beach and a strip of trees separating the land from the nearby buildings of a village. A few people wandering around and little children running around some tall structure, like a watchtower. I was about to wave my hand when I saw a triangular fin from the side, several dozen meters away, which disappeared immediately. I dove upside down. Something loomed from above, for a moment blocking the sun's rays shining on me, refracted by the water. A shadow passed over me. I looked up. Shark - it reached me.

I moved slowly towards the gap that was not far away.

Just don't panic, I was telling myself. Just don't panic.

I started finning the water like crazy. I made it at the last minute because I was happy to find that the fins and feet were in place. It's good that I didn't go further, because it would be after me. I squeezed through the crack to the other side, where Leon was already waiting for me, looking at watch. I grabbed his arm and pulling upwards we came to the surface. He must have noticed something on my face because he asked what was wrong.

We're back on the ship, quick. Sharks! We waved at the dinghy as we climbed at it, I grabbed the helmsman's radio and called:

"Bill, shoot the rockets, the sharks are around!"

"You are all safe and sound," she adds with satisfaction.

"But we did not see anything, and we carefully observe the surface!" the helmsman explains.

"Please tell us everything again," we ask Mona. We are sitting in the wardroom. Coffee and hot cakes smell delicious, and somehow we can't believe at those sharks.

"Wait, how did little Luisa's mother say?" Mona says again. "Don't go over there," she was saying to me. "It's bad terrain. You can fall asleep there."

"Maybe not fall asleep but die or get killed?"

"These cow remains, crates and sharks tell you nothing?" Bill asks.

"Crates in metal cages and they are not rusted, so they are often used. For what?"

"Drugs! Cocaine, guns or whatever," Keys breathes out triumphantly.

She has always been good at associating facts.

"They store drugs there, and the sharks are there to scare people like us. Cows to eat because they are in a closed water. Those who attacked us had to somehow escape. Do you remember that big storm a few days ago? Maybe then they broke out of that basin."

"We're going out of here. Better to have nothing to do with the Colombian drug cartel. Remember in the port, say that we were not on the Goddess of Dreams, but nearby, on the Isle of Lovers. It's a small piece of land, a headland, not an island, but that's how it was named hundreds of years ago and has a pretty cool legend associated with it," I'm talking to them.

In the evening, we were having dinner in a nearby restaurant, when Luisa came up to Mona again.

Mona gave her a few dollars and a giant doll she had previously bought at the store.

But the little one did not come here for that.

She discreetly handed Mona the paper.

"Run!" only that was written on it.

Within fifteen minutes "Shell" was on its way to the open sea - away from this charming, but as it turned out, not always safe port. Four hours later an unmarked helicopter flew over us, making a circle over us and turned towards land.

Returning to Canada, we stopped in many interesting places, watching life on the reefs and honing our skills of underwater treasure hunters. Bill was throwing an old anchor into the water, which had four metal worn buoys attached to short chains of one meter, which went with it to the bottom. We were supposed to find it using our sonar, an underwater search camera and the navigation data it provided.

While at anchor in a small bay in Bermuda, I was supplying Keys with fresh meat in the form of caught fish and squid.

In the morning, when everyone was still asleep and Keys went to kitchen, I went out to the aft deck to ditch my hook with fish bait. I didn't wait long for the first prey this morning - with great difficulty using mine long hooked landing net, I hauled shark on deck. It was not big, about five feet.

It was a harmless species from the local Bermuda Bay. I was glad - there will be a fresh steak for dinner.

I dressed it, cutting only the delicate flesh from the side of its back, and threw the rest into a special hermetic basket. At least I thought so. We had four such trash cans. One for food, one for plastics, the third for cans and bottles, and the fourth on paper. It was an iron rule not to throw any food waste in the place where we dived - this was only done on the high seas. I took the fillets to the kitchen.

During her morning coffee, Mona screamed into the wardroom. And we drank coffee at ten.

"What's that doing there?!" She points to the stern with her hand. We walk curious about what upset her so much.

Even Keys came out of her kingdom.

At the end of the stern, where I was fishing in the morning, next to the bollard was the severed head of a shark I had caught. His gills were still moving rhythmically.

"When did you catch it?" Leon asked.

"In the morning, around six."

"They are vital!" he said.

"This is a warning from the Colombian Mafia," I joked. Taking a long hook, I grabbed his eye and threw him into the bucket.

"I don't think you are going to eat it," Mona says in a surprised voice, looking around for support.

"I will and why not? It will not be cannibalism, this species is harmless to people," I said calmly.

"The steaks are almost ready," Keys said. "There will be fries for that. What, should I not do?" She asks us with hope in her voice.

"Do, dinner will be tasty," said the steersman.

Keys sighed and headed for the kitchen.

# Chapter X

## Search

*Thursday, November 18*

The return of "Shell" from Bermuda took fourteen days. And the whole trip was thirty-six. You had to come back, because some people were running out of holidays. Keys as well.

Leon and Mona got off in Miami, Florida, from where they had booked tickets to Naomi. They had no time to go any further.

Ryszard and Keys was so close to each other that the question of whether they would continue together would be completely tactless.

But they both - each of them separately - asked it each other.

"What now? There is still some time until summer in Canada," Ryszard thought. He decided to talk seriously with Keys about it.

Whole sequences of sentences fell between them about their feelings, especially Keys liked to talk about how much she loved him. But he was more reserved on this point. Yes - he declared that he felt also very good, but deep down he did not know what to do next.

He didn't want to live in this cold part of Canada and Keys couldn't imagine a life away from her native Naomi.

"How to reconcile it?" Keys asked as they passed Cape Chidley and Ungavat Bay appeared over the horizon leading to Naomi.

"Stay with me, we'll be fine," she asked.

"I'll stay until my contract departure." They asked him from Petronafta to finish the contract for some sick Russian, "and then we will decide what to do next. It will be winter soon, and when I come back from this less than two-month voyage, it will be spring and we will set off to search in early summer. Then I'll try to find a job here and we'll buy a house."

It was his first declaration that he would stay with her here in Canada. Her heart leapt into her throat with emotion.

She was waiting for her engagement ring, and he knew it. Jacqueline told him just before going to the Caribbean:

"Keys think the world of you. Don't hurt her like that Harry."

"Gregor's mate from the ship?" He asked.

"Do you know about him?"

"Yes, Keys told me he hurt her a lot, but nothing else."

Jacqueline came up to him from across the room, gently took his hands in hers and looking him in the eyes, said:

"Keys, contrary to appearances, is very sensitive."

"I know that," he said.

"And he broke off the engagement three weeks before the wedding, told her he changed his mind. For almost two years, until she met you, she wasn't seeing anyone."

What he didn't know was that Keys had recently asked Jacqueline:

"What do you think, little sister, will Richard propose to me in the Caribbean?"

"I don't know, baby, these are your business. But he's okay. I know he didn't have any girlfriend in Poland, he cried in my sleeve when he told about it. I told you about it," she reminded.

"Krzysztof, his friend, told me the same!"

And glad she was the one, she hugged Jacqueline heartily.

They came back from the Caribbean, and he ran away from her, tucked his tail like a dog, and ran out to sea, he marched in Philadelphia. He was gone for almost two months, which he broke under one of the oil rigs in the Gulf of Mexico. He came to Naomi in the bloom of spring orchids and greenery that pierces here and there.

He brought Keys what she cared most about. The assurance that his going to sea was a mistake he made because he was afraid. He was afraid of stabilization and life here on land, but now he knows that only she is important and he will be where their home is.

A great welcoming celebration organized by Keys in the "Northern Lights" rented for this occasion gathered all friends of Richard and Keys and their families. Keys was greatly surprised when, two days after his arrival from Rio, he informed her:

"We're going to the airport. We have guests from Poland. My mother arrives, accompanied by Krzysztof."

It surprised her a bit because he hadn't spoken to her about it. Yet they talked every day during all the days he was at sea.

Seeing the surprise on her face, he said to her in a soft voice:

"On this special day of my return to you, I would like someone from me to come."

"Of course Ryszard, I am very happy to see them. It is also very important for me to get to know your mother and your friend."

The ceremonial meeting on Tuesday gathered so many guests that the place was only at their disposal. Of course, there was also everybody from "Shell", and many of the invited guests Ryszard did not even know.

In the evening, when everyone was seated at the tables, Keys was happy to have Richard with her, got up and went to the podium to greet everyone. She was about to leave when Ryszard unexpectedly approached her. He stood next to her, grabbed her hand and said hello to everyone, introduced them to his mother and Krzysztof, thanked all the guests for coming, and finally said:

"But that's not the only reason I came in here," and he did something unexpected."

He knelt in front of Keys.

"Will you be my wife?" He said to her. "I love you and I want to spend the rest of my life with you."

Keys stood enchanted, stared in surprise at Ryszard on his knees, his hand extended towards her, in which he was holding a box with an engagement ring.

"Yes, yes..." she said softly, only to scream loudly in a moment "I love you!" She threw herself on his neck. They kissed, ignoring the thunderous applause.

The rest of the evening, due to its beginning, was marked by their engagement.

The next few days, Ryszard lazed about.

He always did after returning from contract. He only took care of his mother, and Krzysztof, who, due to his work, could not stay as long as he wanted, returned to Poland.

"She's worth it," he said to Ryszard, not embarrassing the fact that Keys was standing next to him.

"And you are worth Ryszard," she replied, kissing him on the cheek. "Don't worry, we'll be visiting you often."

For now, Ryszard lived with Keys, and his mother took the guest room upstairs. To their surprise, she preferred to spend her days with Jacqueline, where little M... and K... taught her the English she had forgotten, and she repaid by playing with them and taking long walks.

Spring has come to Naomi for good, and with it Ryszard's mother missed home.

"Beloved, it's time for me, I would like to return to my country. I'm fine with you, but you know you don't "replant old trees"."

They drove her to the airport and brought her, crying, to the terminal.

It took Ryszard the next two weeks to consider what he would like to do here.

"You can do whatever you want. But don't leave me for that long," Keys pleaded. "I don't have as much time as you."

It made him wonder about her "as long as you do", but thought he had misunderstood her.

"But I know nothing only what I have done so far..."

"Not true! You are perceptive, determined, you like the sea... You could work in the port.

Either run your own business, such as a marine store, or get employment in the local marine rescue service."

"I think the last one would suit me best." He agreed with Keys.

She said nothing to him, but she was very happy because she worried that Ryszard was looking for an excuse to return to his contracts.

What is her dear little sister for? She thought, and secretly from Ryszard shared the news with her. Jacqueline went to work with the energy of a "manager", looking for someone among her friends who would help Ryszard to work there.

In the evening, Bill came over to see them. In fact, he wanted to talk to Keys and Richard about their search, but they got lost somewhere and didn't answer the phone. Yet they made an appointment with him today.

As always, the darkest place is under the candle. When Jacqueline complained to Bill that Ryszard would like to work in a Marine Rescue and she doesn't know how to help him, Bill simply said:

"Wait a minute."

He took the phone and called somewhere.

"Hello, old friend, how are you?" She heard. They talked about family and the weather, and then Bill asked:

"Have you heard of Richard? What saved people on our submarine?" He waited a moment. "Would there be a place for him with you? He's staying in Canada, he has a nice girlfriend and he's looking for a job. Okay, until later," he added after a long moment. "Me too."

Then, calmly as if nothing had happened, he said to Jacqueline:

"Have him prepare the papers and go there for interviews. They will be waiting for him."

"How's that?" Jacqueline was surprised and sat down in the chair, coffee in hand.

The head of sea rescue is my colleague from good sea years. I ate a barrel of salt with him, he will not deny me anything. As soon as it becomes formally possible, Richard is bound to get somewhere.

"What are you guys talking about?" Keys asked, walking into the living room with Ryszard.

"About your search expedition," Jacqueline informed her.

"We just brought the logbook from the bank. Get Gregor and sit down to this Swabian puzzle," Ryszard said, spreading the maps and U-boat Captain's letter on the table.

"Bill, open a journal on a page a few days earlier and look for clues about the second U-boat."

Gregor had just come downstairs to them, and Jacqueline was about to sit on his lap and help unfold the maps.

"What do we have?" Bill asked matter-of-factly.

"Nothing," said Gregor.

"Not true - we know that the crates were taken by a second U-boat that he sunk them somewhere, and the information about it is hidden in the captain's journal and letter. That's a lot," Keys replied, her nose stuck to the two documents.

"Yes, Keys is right, the other U-boat took the crates away and returned without them. If we knew how many hours or days he was gone, the search area would narrow," Bill supports Keys.

He picks up the ship's log book and flips the pages backwards, starting on April 13, 1945.

April 13, 1945: "My best navigator has not returned. Otto exclusively explained that there was an accident and he drowned. I don't believe him, the SS probably killed him."

"What is this? Isn't it important?" Jacqueline asks.

"They got rid of the witness who mapped the location of the crates," Keys points out rightly.

April 10, 1945: "We donated all our iron fuel to the U-562. They'll last two or three days. This is all I can give them, the rest must be enough for the journey to Argentina.

I gave him my best navigator - Otto asked for him. Their navigators are rookies with no experience.

No news from Berlin - the capital is under siege."

April 6, 1945: "U-562 with the generals of SS-men entered the base, they said about some ODESSA organization. How did these rookies get here? How did they get in? I was no longer surprised when it turned out that my best listener had been pulled onto their ship."

He kept shifting necks until the U-boat left the Formosa port.

"We have nothing else," he added in a disappointed voice.

"We do," Ryszard said. "We know that they were in the sea for two to three days, that is, the way to hiding the chests is less than a day or a day and a half. Because the return to base is twice as long, and they probably needed some time to sink the crates. Gregor, how many knots did submerged U-boats?"

"Maybe seven to twelve."

Bill took the compass he had prepared, stuck it on the map, marked a secret base, and made the first semicircle 268 miles in radius. Then he made a second semicircle with a radius of 332 miles.

"This is an area where they could hide the chests. Now we mark out with a green pen the places where it is too deep to do this. And so we have a lot of places to search," he said dissatisfied.

"It's too easy to be true, and it's still looking for a needle in a stream," Ryszard changed a proverb that was known in Poland a little bit, because they certainly did not know what a haystack was.

"It's a good few miles to the left and right of a secret base, and quite a bit of Greenland from both the Labrador Sea and the Greenland Sea," added Keys, staring intently at the map. But she doesn't give up that easily.

"Canada is not grasped by this area," she says pensively. "Why?" She wonders.

"Greenland is a wasteland, I guess that's why," Bill has his theory.

"Gregor, we're not going to come up with anything so dry. The more that we have to look in the water," Richard turns to his brother-in-law.

"Black Jack" appears on the table, and Jacqueline is skillfully juggling an ice canister and five whiskey glasses.

Keys reads the captain's farewell letter intently.

"What is the clue here?" She mutters to herself. "For those who will one day discover our Secret Base" this is the first clue" she says and quotes us from the letter.

"He was aware that someone would discover their base someday. He also knew that his wife would never receive the letter."

So this letter to wife is just an excuse to convey some important information to those "who will discover our Secret Base one day". We know that it is about chests and their national treasure.

But why did he not write directly where they hid it? She whispers in an undertone more to herself than to us.

"Do you think of something?" she interrupts her monologue.

"I think he was afraid, for example, of the third U-boat, who was not privy to the SS-men escaping to Argentina, and knew this place because he was already here," Gregor shares his observations.

"That may be the case, but I think he was more afraid that his plan would fail and others would take possession of the crates."

"It doesn't really matter why he encrypted these messages," Bill settles the argument. "You have to find the key to the position where they hid the crates."

"How did you say? Position? This is the keyword: position!" Ryszard said.

Bill got it right away, but the rest didn't.

Keys also took what was going on, for she immediately started staring at the letter, saying aloud:

"There's a hidden "position" here somewhere. The longitude and latitude are a row of numbers. Only what?" She asks, staring at Ryszard.

"Longitude is given in degrees in three digits and latitude in two digits. To this you need to add minutes and seconds, also in two-digit notation.

So the length is seven or six digits and the width is six digits. Except that the length notation may or may not precede 0."

"What is the position of the Secret Base?"

Bill hands her the position.

"Give me a card quickly." He writes down the position of the Secret Base, then reads aloud:

"However, they will not get there after they boasted that 63 prisoners of war of various nationalities were murdered here. They were building this secret base fortieth year. The SS men murdered them forty-first year. It was 32 Russians from Królewiec and 21 Poles from Gdańsk, the rest are Norwegians from Alesung - all prisoners from Stutthof."

"Is it length or width?" he asks and writes 63o41'40 ".

"That's the length," says Bill, and adds N, so we have 63o41'40 " N.

Bill traces the given length on the map.

"And where is W, width? It makes no sense and puts you in no position in this area and probably in any other area," Bill is feverish.

"Relax, it's not over. Fill me up, I'll think better," Keys jokes.

Ryszard had already guessed what she was up to. But she figured it out, so let her continue.

"As you can see," she took a long gulp, "we used all the numbers in the letter. We still miss a lot of them."

"So where do you get the rest?" Gregor asked.

"From the letter, dear sister-in-law, from the letter!"

"The numbers 63, 41, 40 are not related to anything, while 30 and 21 are related to the names of the cities. They also have their position on the maps. In my opinion, this is where you should look for the missing numbers."

Bill threw himself on the maps looking for Europe.

"Here, write," Keys quickly gave the missing numbers.

"Well, we have position!" Keys triumphantly concluded her investigation. It wasn't too difficult, but the captain didn't have much choice, and probably not the time either.

"Beloved," said Ryszard, "it will be difficult anyway, because remember that in 45 there was no radar or GPS, and the positions were taken using a sextant, which is tantamount to the possibility of making a mistake, because we do not know if they took it in day or night, whether the sky was shining or cloudy. I hope they left a mark on the ground, because they knew about these difficulties themselves, and yet they killed the navigator, deciding that they would no longer need," added.

Bill's map position was a small island near Nuuk, Greenland, 276 miles from the Secret Base.

"So when are we leaving?" Keys asked.

We spent the rest of the evening discussing the details of the expedition and speculating what would happen if there was gold or some works of art in the chests.

"They'll take everything from us or give us sop?" Gregor wondered. "Let William explain to us what we can and what is forbidden by law," he added.

"Whose law?" I asked. "Canadian because we are Canadians, Danish because it is Danish territory or German as the historical heir to Nazi Germany?"

"We have a dilemma then," Jacqueline sighed heavily.

"We will not count one's chickens, whatever will be, will be, and William will explain it best when we come across something," Keys is settling the dispute.

We finally set a date - mid-July. Summer is in full swing, there will be no more snow maybe we can find some tips on land.

Our whole gang is back together on "Shell". This time we have a clearly defined goal: to find the chests. Three days' journey, and therefore three, because "Shell" was faster than "Medusa" and swallowed faster the distance separating us from the position set by Bill.

A small cross on the map greeted us with the stark scenery of the rocky shores of this small island. We swam around it three times, probing the depth of the bottom. Only two places near the cross were suitable for sinking these chests. In other places it would be their graveyard due to the depth. At least for the technology that was available in 1945.

Gregor invited Big Ear to the expedition. It was supposed to tell us in which places the submarine could maneuver freely, getting rid of these crates.

However, we did not know how big the crates were or what they were made of.

The only clue was the two thin, rectangular concrete sarcophagi found in the Secret Base.

"It must have served them for something. I think they hid the crates in them and poured concrete over the top and then flooded it. Otherwise, why would these handles be mounted on their sides?"

"You're right, I think so too," I support Keys, looking at the photos of these concrete blocks with a magnifying glass in my hand.

Our camera is already in the water and we are swimming back and forth scanning the bottom. So far, we haven't discovered anything, but this is just the beginning.

Big Ear through binoculars is scanning the shore. We wonder what he is looking for there.

The marked position is about two or three hundred meters from the shore. Even with a mistake in plotting it on the chart, they couldn't have been wrong about the depth. They certainly coped well with this and did not throw the crates into the 200-meter depth.

On the third day of fruitless search Big Ear communicates to us in the morning:

"Before you start those crazy turns of yours, I'd like you to get closer to these rocks. I have to check something."

We all go out to the aft deck. In the distance you can see steeply protruding rocks rising out of the land like miniature pillars of Heracles. We drop the pontoon onto the water and the three of us sail along the shore.

"Something looked unnatural to me here," says Big Ear. "I watched the shore at noon and noticed nothing. It was only in the evening, while lying in the bunk, that I realized that I saw something unnatural, something that should not be there. These were the rocks in front of us. But what was that?" He moans softly to himself.

We all stare at the great, protruding boulders pushed out of the center of the earth by the wrathful forces of nature many millions of years ago.

"I got it!" He calls. "Look at the third one from the left. Swim a little to the right to be exposed by this boulder in front of us," he says to the helmsman.

"I don't see anything extraordinary about them."

"And I think I do," he says to me, glued to the binoculars. "To the shore! We'll find out soon."

We went ashore, guided by Big Ear exactly where he wanted.

"Now you see?" he asks.

"We can't see anything. Tell me what's going on!" Gregor was angry.

"The other boulder was shot at by some cannon! It could only be a U-boat."

We walk two hundred meters to the very boulder.

He is right! Absolutely right. The sides of the boulder are torn out by bullets, and its front wall has several depressions from explosions.

"It's been many years, so the color is not very different, but if we did a good search, there must be some fragments," he convinces us, staring intently into the ground.

"No need, this is the mark they left. For sure!"

I speak to Bill on the radio:

"Set the "Shell" so that you have both boulders in one line. Underneath, at the bottom, there are crates."

We returned to the "Shell". They were at the bottom and waiting for us. The camera clearly showed eight rectangular blocks scattered along the line to the boulders.

Bill dropped the anchor.

"Leon and Mona are going down into the water," he ordered. "Depth: less than twenty meters. You hook up one crate and we pull it out."

In less than an hour, the first crate was on board. Overgrown with black shells, with no handles that had rusted, and wrapped by Leon in steel ropes, it lay at the stern and blew everyone away with the secret of its contents.

I was on the bridge when I heard a loud shout:

"Keys overboard!!!" The helmsman shouted. I jumped on the wing. It was about five or six meters from our side. But I can see that she is not flowing, but is slowly sinking into the water. I jumped off the wing as I was standing. I was overwhelmed by the bitter cold as I submerged myself completely in the water. The thermal shock blocked my airways and I couldn't catch my breath. But when I went to Keys, the adrenaline overcame my body's resistance and I was quickly at the point where I last saw her. Out of the corner of my eye, I noticed someone in a thermal suit jumping into the water. I dove. I noticed the white Keys smock some distance away from me. I swam desperately towards it. I knew I only had a minute, maybe one and a half and I will need help myself. I swam over to her, grabbed her unconscious body by the collar of her smock and pulled up. I felt my hands stiffen with the cold.

As long as I don't let her go - I think on my way to the surface. I swim out, and my lungs, like a blacksmith's bellows, draw air. The lifebuoy is a meter from me. With the last of my strength, I swim towards it, holding Keys head high above the water. I tuck the wheel under her back and hold it in both hands, hugging Keys from the front. Her eyes are closed. I wonder if she's breathing, but I'm afraid to let go of that round orange piece of plastic to check it out because I may not have the strength to tighten my hands on it again. I feel my whole body begin to go numb from the cold. I don't feel my legs anymore. I had time to think where the pontoon was when I saw Leon's frightened face. He grabbed Keys from behind and tossed her up. They hauled her up on the pontoon, and with their help I landed right behind her.

After a minute she was in the wardroom, on the table. I was lying on the aft deck and I was slowly recovering, shaking like the proverbial jelly.

"What about Keys?" I ask Leon, who undresses me and rubs my whole body. They put me on a stretcher wrapped in two blankets and carry me to the wardroom. I hear Bill calling on the satellite phone on the emergency channel:

"Mayday! Mayday! I have a sick person, I need a doctor immediately!" then gives our position.

Mona gives me some liquid and I ask:

"Is she breathing?"

"She's breathing, I think it's a stroke. She is sick, very sick."

The Mona's words hit me like a bolt from the blue.

"Keeeys siiiick? What?" I asked, stuttering from chattering my teeth.

"She has a tumor in her brain."

"What!? Nothing that I know of. Why?" I say to her in a trembling voice.

"Because we had to swear to her that we would never tell you about it..."

"Richard, we're lucky! Canadian Marine Rescue helicopter with doctor is already flying from Nuuk, will be there in half an hour!" Bill calls out to me.

I drink some medicine and rub my legs. I feel better now, but I can't get up yet, I have no feeling in them. Mona measure my pulse and blood pressure.

"It's alright Richard, you're back to normal," she says.

She then goes back to Keys, who is lying with an oxygen mask over her face and, listening to the doctor's instructions from the helicopter, gives her some kind of injection.

I am sleepy, very sleepy. I think it's because of the drug Mona gave me. I had to take a nap because the noise of the helicopter woke me up. I felt the tingling slowly stopping, my legs still working fine, so I got up. I was dressed in two warm tracksuits and a thick diving sweater. It's Leon or maybe Mona dressed me while I slept. I push myself to the aft deck shouting:

"Keys! Keys, I'm going with you!"

A helicopter maneuvers over me, keeping a steady position above our stern. A doctor stopped me.

"I've already taken care of you, you'll be fine, but she needs to get to the hospital as soon as possible."

He hooked the harness to the hook and flew up. I was left alone. I stood for a long time watching him disappear in the distance a helicopter.

I entered the wardroom with a heavy heart. At the entrance I was greeted by a grave mood. The vague expressions told me Keys was bad. I sat down next to Mona, who put her arm around me.

"Richard, you did more than you could..."

"What happened?" I ask, looking at Leon.

"I don't know, nobody knows how Keys got in the water. I heard the helmsman scream, then a splash and saw you swimming, so I quickly jumped into my suit and jumped into the water after you.

You were quick and you disappeared under the water for a long time, I didn't know exactly where you were going to swim, but you appeared with Keys next to the wheel the steersman had thrown. That's it, you know the rest."

"I think I know how it happened," Mona said softly, not looking my way. "I saw vomit next to the garbage cans. That's probably why Keys got outside and then she had to pass out and fall overboard."

"Why on earth was she throwing up?!" I asked.

"She was very sick, she took medications that worked that way sometimes."

"Why am I the last to know about this?!" I look at each of them in turn.

"Keys wanted it so. She asked us not to tell you anything," says Mona.

"She had... You know..." the word "cancer" wouldn't go through my throat - "tumour"? I finally blurted out the hated word.

"No, Richard. When Keys was a child, she was diagnosed with an inoperable lump, some sort of hematoma in the brain. It grew with her. The diagnosis was unequivocal and did not change over the years - you can live with it a day, a hundred years or turn into a plant in an instant."

The world swirled before my eyes.

Meanwhile, "Shell" returned to Naomi with all the power of its engines. I was wondering how I would survive the three days at the port. The next morning we got a call from Jacqueline that Keys was in a Toronto hospital and her condition was stable.

"Book a plane for me," I asked.

"Yes, of course, Richard. The ticket will be waiting for you."

Two days was a nightmare of sleepless nights and a sea of drank coffee, and finally Mona gave me some pills.

"Take it and don't talk," she said firmly, and made sure I swallow them.

Jacqueline is waiting for us on the quay, all dressed in black. We are going with Gregor towards her. I have a heart in my throat and chase the thought away.

When we were quite close, we heard her burst into tears instead of saying hello.

"Keys is dead... She died right after my call two days ago..."

I don't remember much of what happened in the next week. A funeral, a funeral banquet then I lay numb for three days in our bed with my clothes on, empty vodka bottles littered next to me. Finally Jacqueline appeared.

"Richard, you can't live like that, buck up. She wouldn't want you to despair. Take care of yourself. Keys knew she was going to die, she had lived with this thought since she was a child. She was very happy to meet you. You made her life's dream come true by taking her to the Caribbean."

"Why didn't I know about this?"

"She didn't want this. She begged us not to tell you anything. She wanted to live like a normal person."

"Jacqueline, why didn't she tell me about her illness herself?"

"She was scared."

"What?"

"She thought you would leave her when you found out about it. So did her previous boyfriend, Gregor's friend Harry. The one who died on the submarine. When she told him how sick she was after their engagement, he broke up with her saying, "I only have one life - forgive me," and left her. It was almost two years ago," she added.

Before leaving for Poland, I went to cemetery.

"Keys... I wouldn't leave you, I loved you..." I was talking to her in my mind.

After two weeks, I received a short message from Bill in my e-mail. As usual, documented with photos.

"There are books in the chest, Hitler's Mein Kampf and a strange map signed as "ODESSA". It belonged to one of the SS men who "took care" of the diamonds. Five thousand carats received in the last days of the war, for the needs of this organization, it was marked on this map, only that I do not understand anything about it, but the trail leads to Poland.

The question is:

"What's next?"

Reading this, I heard Hans chuckle in my head, the captain of the U-boat.

Bill's next step was to send me the map, but this time not via the Internet, but by a special courier "to my own hands". The secret it was hiding was too valuable to risk sending it via internet mail.

I did not think then that all of our team would soon meet in Poland and begin a further search for valuables hidden by the Nazis, which were to end up in their secret organization, Odessa.

www.ingramcontent.com/pod-product-compliance
Lightning Source LLC
LaVergne TN
LVHW010614100826
845148LV00014B/2963